THE GOOD TIME

Also by Nell Stevens

Non-Fiction

Bleaker House

Mrs Gaskell & Me

Fiction

Briefly, A Delicious Life

The Original

THE GOOD TIME

NELL STEVENS

SCRIBNER EDITIONS

London · New York · Amsterdam/Antwerp · Sydney/Melbourne · Toronto · New Delhi

First published in Great Britain by Scribner Editions,
an imprint of Simon & Schuster UK Ltd, 2026

1 3 5 7 9 10 8 6 4 2

Simon & Schuster UK Ltd, 1st Floor, 222 Gray's Inn Road
London WC1X 8HB

Simon & Schuster Australia, Sydney
Simon & Schuster India, New Delhi

www.simonandschuster.co.uk
www.simonandschuster.com.au
www.simonandschuster.co.in

The authorised representative in the EEA is Simon & Schuster Netherlands BV, Herculesplein 96, 3584 AA Utrecht, Netherlands. info@simonandschuster.nl

A CIP catalogue record for this book is available from the British Library

Hardback ISBN: 978-1-3985-3341-7
eBook ISBN: 978-1-3985-3342-4
Audio ISBN: 978-1-3985-5427-6

Printed and Bound in the UK using 100% Renewable Electricity at CPI Group (UK) Ltd

FSC www.fsc.org MIX Paper | Supporting responsible forestry FSC® C013604

For Leslie Epstein, 1938–2025

CONTENTS

The Minutes

1.

10 March 2013

We are waiting for Peter to get here so the meeting can start. There's a bad atmosphere in the room – something between Kat and Adam, I think – and I've volunteered to take the minutes so I can keep my head down, typing.

Location: Kat's flat, a low-ceilinged new-build place in Peckham, where everything feels too close together and tuneless singing strains through the walls: the neighbours are holding a prayer circle. Occasional shouts of 'Amen!' and 'Praise Jesus!' punctuate the droning.

Present: Kat, on the floor, her legs stretched out under the glass coffee table and her elbows resting atop it; Diya, curled up on the sofa, reading; Adam, at the main table, scrolling on his phone and pretending not to be furious about whatever it is Kat has done or not done that he is furious about. Now Peter has arrived and is already talking too loudly, and everyone is gathering around the coffee table. Diya pours wine into tumblers. Kat spreads her hands over the table's glass surface, as though she's trying to smooth out a crease, and says, 'Let's get into it, then.' When she shifts her legs, a flake of mud falls away from the sole of her shoe, like a stray puzzle piece. The meeting starts.

Apologies – or rather, conspicuous lack of apology – from: you.

Item 1: the dismantling of our exhibition of squatters' art. The show is housed in an abandoned building with boarded-up windows – it used to be a pub – and the plan was for the exhibition to be ousted, forcibly, by the landlord, hopefully in the presence of a photographer, and that the record of this eviction would then form the basis of a subsequent display. Except that the landlord has failed to notice the presence of the squatters' art in his property for two months, so the anticipated expulsion has not taken place, and we all have more pressing things to do than continue to man the exhibition, especially since everyone who was ever going to visit came to the private view, and hasn't returned. Term is about to start: the final term of our final year of university; we need to spend more time in the library and less time supervising the exhibition. We will have to take the art down ourselves.

'Or we could just leave it there,' says Diya, 'and see what happens to it over time. It might fall down, or get stolen, and we can keep a record, take photos of it, the death of art.'

Peter objects to the concept of treating art as disposable.

Adam agrees with Peter, and says we should at least notify the artists that they can collect their work.

Diya: 'We could ask if they were willing to donate the

works to a project examining artistic decay. What happens to a painting nobody looks at? That sort of thing.'

Peter, glancing across at me, at my fingers on the keyboard: 'Diya's suggestions are noted in the minutes. Thanks, Diya.'

I nod and underline Diya's original thought about the death of art. Diya sighs; a storm is brewing, an argument about the boys talking over the girls, dismissing our contributions (and I'm noting this down, too, then switch *boys* to *men* and *girls* to *women*, then back again because it stuck me as pretentious and not particularly accurate) and it seems extraordinary that the boys, the men, the boys, whatever, can't feel it, or don't care.

Your absence is unfortunate. Without you we all feel sheepish and self-conscious and therefore more irritable. Just a bunch of students with nothing better to do than – what was it Leah said before she resigned from the group? – 'pretend that affected stunts and the parroting of half-baked political ideologies is a valuable artistic contribution'. This is why we were all so pleased when you turned up at one of our meetings. Leah, a founding member, had lost patience and abandoned ship, leaving the rest of us feeling rudderless, suddenly unsure what the hell we were doing. Or that was how I felt, and guessed the others did. Then you came along, and things felt clear again. We could never admit it, but it added gravitas, protected us against criticisms like Leah's, to have a bona fide local on our team. *We are a group of young artists based in South London, with an interest in urban exploration, subversive design, art as activism and supporting marginalised communities.* Without you, we were idealistic, self-aggrandising, pretentious. With you, we're endorsed: the real deal.

(Your absence is a shame, too, because I like to catch your eye sometimes during meetings like these and feel that we're laughing at the same thing, that you and I both know this is all a bit ridiculous, the death of art, the un-evicted squatters' exhibition, but also quite moving, how much we all care; how, at the bottom of everything, we really do think art saves lives. So little difference, really, between us and the faithful praying on the other side of the wall.)

Item 2, the only other item, is what we can do to protest, or at least bear critical witness to, the demolition of the Waderley Tower block by the roundabout near the university.

Peter glances around and then asks, sharply, where you are.

A fact lost on nobody: you used to live in Waderley. You grew up on the thirteenth floor, knew its views, smells, the various vibrations of footsteps in the stairwell according to which storey they were passing. It's embarrassing to say it but I was shocked – first shocked, and then, perhaps worse, impressed – when, as we passed the tower block on the bus one day, not long after we first met, on our way to a demonstration against tuition fees, you pointed up to some indeterminate point on the building's flank and said, 'That's my dad's place.'

The building looked so hostile; you are always so warm.

They've razed everything around the tower already. The Waderley Estate used to encircle the roundabout, a big grey nest around a big grey egg. Now, the other buildings are gone: the long concrete walkways, the walls polka-dotted with satellite dishes. Too much crime and not enough community spirit, the council thought: *An area of extremely high social disadvantage.* Too expensive to renovate, to coax back into respectability. Better, they decided, to reduce it to rubble, and then to nothing; to build a shopping centre where it used to be, and luxury flats on top of the shopping centre. The university was thrilled by the plans and did nothing to stop them. All that remains is the tower: a solitary watchman presiding over all this empty space, pits gaping in the ground and scaffolding already going up.

Our group has discussed the demolition before. I've noticed a certain deferral to you when we talk about it. We have already done our best to prevent the eviction of residents, have unfurled all the usual banners – *'PEOPLE BEFORE PROFIT, RENT IS THEFT'* – have written blog posts and erected a petition stand outside the library and started hashtags. But the people are gone now. Your father has been rehoused in an outer borough. The windows are blank, and there are loops of barbed wire strung all over the walls like the Christmas lights around the university buildings, though it is January and they should have been taken down.

That day on the bus, as we juddered around an assault course of roadworks and you directed my eyes up at the tower, I was so interested in you: in the fact that you'd grown up right here in this place that is now my home, too, at once familiar and still a little strange to me, and that from here you'd gone so far away, to the States, to get your masters; that you'd come back to do your PhD at our university, and for some reason wanted to spend time with us, with me, with a bunch of undergraduates avoiding studying by littering the campus and its environs with art and slogans; that you were receptive and helpful when I ranted about my classes, my teachers, my essays, and then, afterwards, I'd check my phone and see that while we were talking, you were also posting a multi-tweet thread about the facility of Komodo dragons to have virgin births. How do you do that, I want to know; how do you live in all these worlds at once? You have tens of thousands of Twitter followers and they all seem as fascinated by you as I am.

Soon after you told me about Waderley, one of my housemates took acid and set fire to the kitchen. You and I decided to live together. We moved into a flat by Burgess Park with one bedroom, and we took turns sleeping in the bed.

I am supposed to be taking the minutes, and if I was doing a good job of it, I'd be able to clear up the dispute that has now arisen about who came up with something that has been named, instantly, 'the Ascension of Waderley'. But my mind wandered – I was thinking about you, about the flat, about whether you'd mentioned this morning that you wouldn't be at the meeting – and suddenly Diya and Kat are both shouting at Peter and Adam, and Peter and Adam are leaning back, arms crossed, smirking at each other, and all I can do is type frantically and catch nobody's eye.

Here's what I've been aware of, at the edges of my attention: someone saying, 'Imagine what it would look like if, when the demolition began, the bricks went up instead of down. Imagine if it looks like Waderley's ascending.'

Someone else – a male voice? – 'Think of it this way: if Waderley were an animal, it would be a pigeon.' And then, somehow, a collective vision of Waderley filled with pigeons, the birds the exact colour of its walls, and the dust billowing outwards as the building starts to collapse, the birds surging up so it looks as though the bricks have sprouted wings and are flying away. The Ascension of Waderley.

Diya: It's unacceptable for you to take credit for this.

Peter: What exactly do you think you have contributed here?

Me: It would kill the pigeons.

Kat: She contributed the idea, the whole thing.

'It would kill the pigeons,' I say. 'The pigeons would just explode.'

My stomach drops when I think about your hands – as though I'm a child in the back of a car accelerating joyfully over a bump in the road – and the way you fold them around your knees when you're talking to me. Lately you've been doing that – talking to me, holding your knees – while I'm in the bath. You come in and sit on the toilet while I splash about. The air is steamy and you wave your hand in front of your face, as though someone were smoking upwind, which I take as a sort of jokey criticism of my profligate use of hot water. Then you lean back, clutch your legs and tell me about your day. In this way you give the impression you think we are close, or are becoming close, and this thrills me.

You are writing a thesis about Walter Benjamin's *Arcades*

Project, but most of your time is spent wandering around the city trying to find a place where you can work. There's never anywhere. The cafes are crowded with students and prams. The pubs are full of men who ask why you're alone. The library, you say, is oppressive: so many books crammed on the shelves, so many people jostling for desk space. You share oddly angled photos of your workplaces, your failing-to-workplaces, with your followers. The updates come hourly, sometimes minute by minute. You'd forgotten how it is in London, you tweet, after living in the States: how impossible it is to find a place to sit down.

Last week: 'Can I come in?' you asked, because you always do, as you pushed open the door and slid through. 'Guess what I did today?' I turned over onto my front, splashing a bit, and the squeak of my skin against the wall of the tub sounded sort of obscene. 'What did you do?'

I thought you would say what you normally say – 'I tried to get some work done in the British Library, in the Starbucks by Borough station, in the Trafalgar Arms.'

Instead: 'I went to Waderley.' In your mouth the word Waderley sounds different, less reverent than when the rest of us say it.

I pictured you standing on the pavement, staring up at the tower. People would have been annoyed at you blocking the walkway; cyclists would have dinged their bells as they swerved around you in the new bike lane. There had been no photo posted of the tower, no tweet about it, and it seemed therefore like privileged information, like a signal from you that I was different to the rest of your followers, a significant person in your life. I waited for you to tell me how you felt, seeing the upright corpse of your old home.

To sound encouraging but not patronising, I just said, 'Oh yeah?'

You paused, pulling your knees closer, peering over them at your toes curled round the toilet seat. 'I found a way in.'

'In?' I said. 'Like, inside in?'

You nodded. 'There's a way into the building round the back. There are some security cameras but I don't think they're on. All those signs about guard dogs are just for show. I cut through some wire. The back door into the building, where the boiler and the pipes are, it's just open. I walked right in.'

'It's not safe,' I said. 'It might not be structurally sound.' I felt a pang of irritation. I was annoyed to think of you doing this, though I had no evidence the building was dangerous, no specific fear other than something vague and selfish I couldn't name.

Your eyes were wide. You were speaking quickly.

'We should do something in the tower,' you said. 'We should break in again, all of us, and do something before the demolition. Something big. Peter will love it. He'll finally get to be like those people who climbed the Shard. Or the ones who broke into Aldgate Tube at the royal wedding. We'll all go in and we'll find a way to say goodbye to Waderley, something beautiful.'

'What?' I asked.

'I don't know,' you said. 'Make some art. A bigger explosion than the actual explosion.'

'They got ASBOs, those Aldgate Tube people,' I say. 'They weren't allowed to talk to each other for ten years.'

I turned over. Bathwater splashed onto your leg. I sank down so that my ears were underwater, and my own voice sounded explosive in my head when I said, 'Ten years. Imagine not talking for ten years.' I came up and studied your expression.

'We won't have to do that,' you said, and I felt soft again, warm towards you. 'We won't get caught.' I flicked some water at your face and you crowed. You bent over the bath and splashed some back at me, which made me kick, sending water everywhere. At that point you were half-soaked already and I had never been so close to you before, wasn't sure if we'd ever even touched each other by accident, brushing up against each other in the kitchen or anything like that, certainly nothing like this, and we were both laughing and then you jumped in on top of me, fully clothed. Water got into my mouth and made me splutter. You wriggled and kicked. Half the contents of the tub ended up on the floor, and the neighbour on the other side of the wall thumped it a few times, until we shut up. We lay still, tangled limbs and dripping hair, and we panted and listened to the leftover quiet in the room. A bigger explosion than the actual explosion. I had the feeling that if I moved suddenly, or at all, you would vanish.

So it occurs to me now that perhaps it was my idea, the Ascension of Waderley. Or at least, the filtering of your idea, through me, into the conversation, into the minutes.

2.

17 March 2013

Back at Kat's place for another meeting. There was a party here last weekend, and remaining detritus makes it feel as though we're posing for one of the photographs in the squatters' exhibition. It's cold; I'm wrapped in a blanket that was thrown over the side of the sofa. The laptop I'm typing on nestles against the wool, which smells strongly of cheap aftershave and makes me think of the boys I fell in love with in first year, the exaggerated way they used to move their shoulders as they walked, as though they could power their legs from the neck down. They were so impressive to me: solid and desirable. It seems longer than two years ago that I felt that way about them.

You are here, now, though you're busy on your phone and won't look at me.

'We've got the pumps and the balloon samples,' Peter says.

'Uh-huh?' you say, as though he were telling this to you alone, and I want you to be livelier, to be more pleased, because who are we doing this for, why are we doing this, if not for you, if not to please you?

There has been a flurry of messages in the group chat since the last meeting, and the Waderley plan has morphed into something more concrete and – slightly, so slightly that it seems, still, like a punchline to a joke I didn't hear – more realistic.

You: *So just to get this straight, you want to fill the building with pigeons*

Peter: *Yes*

Kat: *The Ascension of Waderley*

You: *But the pigeons would just die*

Me: *That's what I said*

You: *They'd just get blown up with everything else*

Me: *Exactly*

You: *I've seen videos of tower blocks being demolished. They fire a shot first, to scare off birds in the building – and what you're suggesting is that we lock pigeons in a room so they can't escape, and they'll hear that warning shot and start to panic, but they won't be able to get out, it'll be chaos and feathers and screeching and terror and they'll be throwing themselves at the windows, and then the building will explode and that will have been their final living moment*

You were always much more talkative over text than in person.

Peter: *It's unclear that the birds would die*

Me: *They'll definitely die*

You: *Pigeons can detect sounds at lower frequencies than humans. They can hear volcanos and storms from hundreds of miles away*

Peter: *Okay*

Adam: *If we ascertain where, exactly, the explosives will be placed in the building, we can ensure the birds are far away from the sites of the explosions, and just escape when the building begins to disintegrate*

You: *Why not use balloons*

Diya: *Balloons?*

You: *Grey helium balloons*

Me: *Yes, grey helium balloons*

The discussion moved on to the practicalities of balloons, whether the force of the explosion would burst them, and you uttered the words that stopped everyone in their tracks – *as a former resident of the tower* – and you said that if even one grey balloon survived the explosion, if just one brick appeared to float upwards when the building sank down, you'd consider the installation a success.

'Plans are afoot for a Waderley send off (/ up)' you tweeted, and I was proud to know what you meant.

So now here we are. Present: you, me, everyone else. Apologies from no one.

There's a sort of fizzing energy between us that comes in the aftermath of an argument, a new shared purpose, though you seem somewhat immune to it, slumped in the corner: you're frowning, thumbs darting across the bottom half of your phone. We have hired helium pumps from a party shop near Peter's house. Diya and I spent several hours sourcing and ordering various grey balloons online, which Adam now spreads out across the coffee table, an interior designer's swatch of Waderley shades: light, dark, metallic, dull, marbled, translucent, mauve, pigeon-toned. Beside them, Adam places images of the tower. We blow up balloons and compare them to the pictures.

'What do you think?' I ask you, and you just shrug, slide your phone into your pocket, as though even that is boring you now. I check my timeline: you've been arguing with a stranger about whether 'gotten' can be used in British English. 'Forgotten,' you have tweeted. 'Begotten. Misbegotten. Ungotten. Gotten.'

You have been different these past few days: I don't want to say *avoiding me* but it does feel that way. I've been frantically lonely, listening out for your key in the door. I miss you. Perhaps it has been longer that you've been like this: a couple of weeks, since the bath thing, which you've never mentioned, not even to tell me never to mention it, though I've understood that anyway.

We narrow it down to two shades of grey and take a vote.

Yesterday you gave a lecture to my Criticism and Theory class. The timetable read 'BENJAMIN LECTURE' with no speaker listed. I had mentioned to you that it was happening because I thought you'd be interested, and you had nodded and not let on that you'd be the one giving it. Then, on the day, there you were, walking out onto the platform at the front of the room. You tapped the keyboard and the screen above you opened its eye. Black background, white words: THE WORK OF ART IN THE AGE OF MECHANICAL REPRODUCTION and your name underneath in lower case.

The next slide was a photograph of flowers – bulbous crystal vase on a grey surface, petals white and pink and red, the leaves and stalks in muted greens, the palette of something Dutch and old – and underneath it, 'A still from *Big Bang* (2006), Ori Gersht'. You pressed a key and the picture began to move. The vase exploded in slow motion. Red petals splintering out like fragments of coloured glass. Next: video of the video, the same bouquet exploding, playing on several stacked screens running up the side of a tall building. Next:

a quote from Ori Gersht: 'When the explosion happened, you had the sense that that entire building was collapsing.'

Prickle of sweat between my skin and the collar of my shirt. I felt as though this was all for me, supposed to hit me right between the eyes. Then: 'What is the difference,' you asked, 'between a painting, and a photograph of a painting? Between a vase of flowers exploding and a video of a vase of flowers exploding? Between a video of a vase of flowers exploding and a video of a video of a vase of flowers exploding?'

Afterwards, when you had slunk off the stage and we were filing out of the theatre, I felt swelled with pride, fullest of grey balloons, because you had been so casually clever up there and because I knew you. Or, if I didn't really know you, then because you were my person.

I got home later that day to find you eating sunflower seeds at the kitchen table. It was mid-afternoon, not dark yet but thinking about it, the sky just beginning to congeal into something murky, and I was so happy to see you: tangible you who crunched things between your teeth, not the far-off, cool-edged you who had given the lecture, or the cipher of yourself offering opinions on the internet. 'I liked your lecture,' I said. You stood up and the legs of your chair scraped against the floor. You walked to the window. 'Nobody likes lectures,' you said. The tree outside was waving its branches behind your head and it looked for a moment as though you were tangled in it.

'Everyone wanted to be you,' I said and you gave me a look of such offended pity, sorry and wounded and sour.

'Oh, don't start acting your age,' you said, and spat out a striped shell into the palm of your hand.

'I'm interested in those oppositions of attraction and repulsion,' said Ori Gersht, in a slide from the lecture, 'and how the moment of destruction in the exploding mirrors becomes for me the moment of creation.'

The meeting has run long and everyone is tired, losing focus. Peter is playing with the helium pumps, practising filling balloons. He's waving them in your direction, saying, 'This colour is right, right? You're sure this is right?' You're leaning away from him as though you can smell his breath. As you move back, you edge closer to me, and I move my leg out from under the blanket, and wonder whether you'll touch it.

Diya bats a balloon away from her face. 'The demolition is scheduled for noon on Friday,' she says. She points to one of the photos of the building. 'We know there will be simultaneous explosions on different floors, and our best guess is here, and here, and here.'

And this is the plan: we will meet at 2 a.m. on the day of the demolition, take the route that you have already found into Waderley, and divide ourselves into two groups. One set will go to the thirteenth floor, roughly halfway up, use the key you still have to access your father's place, and fill it with balloons. The other will go to the very top floor, force entry into one of the flats there and do the same. Since we don't know exactly where the explosives will be, this seems our safest bet.

'Does everyone know what they're supposed to be doing?' says Peter.

I draw the blanket closer around me and write that the meeting has ended before it has technically ended. My outstretched leg is like a question mark on the floor. You haven't touched it.

It strikes me that everyone in this room is in love with you.

3.

22 March 2013

Location: the barred entrance to the abandoned tower. Waderley is looming blackly overhead, dark lump against velvety, light-polluted sky. Everything seems flat under the street lights; your face in particular looks blank. Darting red edge of Diya's cigarette. We are all wearing hoods. It is Friday. It is 1.59 a.m.

Present, now: all of us except Peter, who texted saying he'd been 'held up' and telling us to go on without him, which means he got drunk and/or lucky, and either way is in bed with no intention of getting out of it. Everyone is annoyed, though it's not the time to get into it, and also embarrassed by how directionless we are without him, without his unquestioning confidence in his own right to take charge. We're all looking at you, waiting for you to tell us what to do.

'Okay?' says Diya, and you mutter, 'Okay.'

Nobody seems to want to move. You say 'Okay' again. I take a deep breath and the smell is damp leaves and petrol and the washing powder you use, which I now use as well.

A motorbike speeds around the roundabout. High-pitched mosquito whine.

You turn to the wire fence that divides the world from Waderley, running your fingers along it, feeling for the break you made before. The wire jangles under your palms.

Diya: Where did you cut it?

You: I'm looking. Give me a second.

Adam: I can't see a hole. They repaired it.

You (mystified): They never repair anything.

But the hole you made is gone, and Kat is fishing wire-cutters out of Adam's bag and handing them to you. You don't react for a moment, just stare at the mesh, and then you take them. You open the jaws of the cutters and close them. You look as though you are gardening, trimming a hedge, but I can smell the metal. You make cuts. The sharp edges of the broken wires catch light from the road. A car hoots its horn but none of us turn to see if it was directed at us; when nothing else happens, you continue. A flap of mesh is loose, now. You peel it back as though it were a page of newspaper and duck through. After you: Kat, Adam, Diya and then me. On the other side, everything seems quieter, even though it can't be.

We file around to the back of the building, moving close to the wall. Security cameras, lights not blinking. I have two of the helium pumps in my backpack and they're clanking against each other as I move; it's almost as though we're going to a party, as though I'm carrying a bag full of cheap booze and we'll turn the corner to find people and noise and not the concrete platform behind the tower, dark.

The door at the back is open, as you said it would be, clanging on its hinges, and we shuffle into the boiler room. As I step inside, I touch the wall and try to imagine that within a day, it won't be there. It seems unmovably solid: the concrete and the litter in the corner of the room and broken glass by the window; the residual smell of cigarettes, rubbish, cannabis.

Through more doorways, torch beams hesitant before us, all of us following you until we reach the stairwell. There's trash and dried leaves on the stairs, rustling as we begin to climb. Four and a half floors up: the bag is heavy and I'm panting. There's a clunk that sounds like a bottle being kicked against a step, and Adam stumbles and yelps. The noise makes us all freeze. Heavy breathing and beyond us, quiet.

Then, somewhere below us, a light comes on. It casts shadows in the stairwell: spidery lines of railings spring up the walls. Adam crouches down at once and the rest of us sink, slowly, fumbling to turn our torches off. We wait. The light downstairs stays on.

There's a thud and then a dog barks, twice. My face is near Diya's leg, which twitches at the sound as though someone has pinched her. Footsteps below us and a voice, echoing up to where we're crouching: 'Through here! This way!'

I inch towards the railings to look over the edge. Two boys, teenagers with a big white dog, are crossing the floor. Paint cans in hand. They've got a large, swaying lamp with them that casts wide shadows. Rattle of ball bearings in aerosol cans. Hiss of paint on the walls. Adam stands up, flicks his torch back on and begins to climb again. Below us, the boys catch sight or sound of him and shout up, 'Who's that? Who's up there?' and then dash back to the exit. Footsteps recede; light fades.

When I look up you're staring at me, smiling. 'You look so scared,' you say, and it's the nicest thing you've said to me in weeks.

There are hundreds of videos of demolitions on the internet. Shaking cameras. Wind buffeting the speakers. A flash and then dust and the sickening lurch of the solid upright thing away from solidness, away from uprightness. Straight lines not straight any more. Sometimes the middle of the building sinks first and the outside walls veer inwards. Sometimes it's the other way round. Sometimes there's a crowd of people who have gathered to watch, and they make 'ahs' and 'oohs' as though they're at a firework display, and then applaud.

We are standing inside your father's old flat. The others have gone up to the top. We've brought head torches. I put mine on and toss one across to you; you grab for it but don't catch it. It rattles on the floor and the batteries roll out. You're still smiling at me as you crouch to put it back together, and it feels like a kind of heat, this shift in your mood. It hasn't been good and easy between us, not since you got in the bath with me and possibly not ever, it just took me a while to notice, but now here you are, and here I am, and we are doing this thing together. You walk to a window and look down at the roundabout, the wreath of red and white car lights around it. I stand next to you for a while, long enough to notice your breaths, which are slower and deeper than mine, and to overthink what I want to say to you, so in the end I say nothing, and return to the task in hand, tipping out balloons from your bag, which you've discarded by the door, and setting up the pumps.

'Here,' I say. 'Come on. Help.'

You turn and raise a hand to shield your eyes from the beam of my torch. Your expression is vague, as though you've forgotten for a moment why we're here. Then you clear your throat and nod. You cross to me.

I watch your fingers as you fit the balloons over the pump's nozzle where the helium comes out, and then release them and knot their necks. Your hands are so busy, twisting and twisting; your face is still.

The pumps hiss and rattle but I stop noticing after a while. We fall into a rhythm of fixing and pushing and tying and letting the balloons float up to the ceiling. I like hearing you beside me, shifting your weight on the floor, sighing; I like the glimpses of your hands at work and the way the smell of laundry detergent is just noticeable over the darker smell of the old flat. Time passes, measured out in taut grey orbs, and soon I'm not even thinking about where we are, or what we're doing, just the rising of the balloons.

It seems, after watching demolition videos, that there should be a way to watch them in reverse. I imagine how they would look on old-fashioned VHS, the way the buildings would re-assemble, leap upwards, soldiers caught slouching on duty. It would seem as though they'd only forgotten themselves for a moment.

But you can't do that on YouTube. I can only click backwards to the moment before the explosion and see it repeat. The present cannot be reconstituted bit by bit into the past. You can only watch the videos forwards, in short bursts, and then again.

I'm thinking about the bath thing. I am constantly thinking about the bath thing, have been spinning out and back to it ever since, through every meeting, through every lecture, through every subsequent bath. Your breath on my breath and how quick you were to jump in. Droplet of water falling on my shoulder from a damp dagger of your hair. It's expanding in my chest and I can't seem to hold it any longer.

'Hey,' I say. 'You know that thing that happened? The bath thing?'

You don't respond. Something feels odd and I glance up. The room is crowded with balloons. They have filled the ceiling and several layers lower, so that there's only a little space above the floor that isn't full. When the beam of my head torch illuminates the grey spheres, they look translucent and murky. I extend an arm to where I guess you are; the balloons creak against each other. My hands grasp air and latex. I can't feel you. After scrabbling around I find the pump you were using. It is lying on its side on the ground.

I reach out around me and begin to feel panicked. Jostling, noisy, the balloons resemble eyes, mouths, eggs.

'Hello?' I say, and my voice sounds echoey. 'Are you there? I think we've done enough. I think we should find the others and go.'

The room doesn't look like a room any more. It feels as though it is already disintegrating. Nothing is familiar; the smell, solid and damp and real when we arrived, has been replaced by the tang of the rubber.

'Hey!' I shout.

I pull my phone out of my pocket to check the time. It is 4 a.m. I call your number and it rings through to a computerised voice saying, 'You have reached the voicemail box of' and then you saying your name. You sound uncertain, as though you're lying. I try twice more, and then stop. Somewhere beyond the tower, sirens are wailing.

I wade through the balloons to the door, and slip out. They nestle on the threshold. I expect to see you in the corridor, but you aren't there, either. I message the group chat, saying I've lost you.

4.

22 March 2013

We are sleepless and fractious and the meeting is convened around a table outside the coffee shop by the roundabout, from where we have a view of the tower. Workers are busying all over it, now, in fluorescent jackets, baubles on a tree. We're supposed to be looking at Waderley but instead I'm looking everywhere for you. Peter is here, hungover and annoyed, saying, 'Right, but where is she?' whenever I try to explain what happened – the room, the balloons, the sudden absence of you – and frowning. 'She can't miss the demolition,' he snaps, and then looks at me and says, 'Put that in the minutes, that she can't miss it,' as though that will make it true.

What I write instead is that I'm scared you're still in the tower. I write that I'm scared we left you behind, that you're stuck somehow, that you can't get out. Or: I'm scared you want to be there, that this was your plan all along. I'm scared that none of us know who you really are or were. I'm scared to check your Twitter feed in case you haven't posted since last night, and I'm scared to check your Twitter feed in case you have, are continuing to tweet, bodylessly and soundlessly from a place I can't reach. Where are you? Why won't you answer your phone?

Places I have not found you:

On the top floor of the tower, where I ran to after leaving your father's flat, and saw that the others had done exactly what we, or I, had done. They'd filled a room with balloons, the same bulging grey. They had been breathing the helium to make their voices squeak, and were giggly and proud of themselves, and Kat and Adam were touching each other and kissing and whatever had been happening between them these past few weeks had finally overflowed, and nobody was really in the mood for me to panic, and they said you must have got bored and left and that it was no big deal.

Outside the tower on the pavement, waiting for us to emerge, smoking a cigarette.

On any of the streets between Waderley and our flat, walking or sitting, or waiting for a bus.

At home, in the bed or on the sofa, or sitting at the table, or standing in the window. I stood there instead and thought that it was not beyond you to be hiding on purpose. You are not above playing tricks on people. You might in fact quite like to be seen to disappear, to be experienced as having disappeared, for a joke, some kind of stunt. But then I thought: it's not beyond you to really disappear, either, to be truly beyond me, beyond yourself. At least I don't think it is. I don't think I know you very well. I don't think I know you at all. Everything in the flat was as we'd left it and I could tell – it seemed clear – that you hadn't been back. In the fridge: half-eaten tray of supermarket sushi. On the floor by the front door: boots you wore to teach in, which you complained rubbed the skin of your heels. Just as it was when we left, except that it suddenly all seemed staged, arranged to look as though people lived there, rather than a place we really lived: an installation.

Here, now, inside or outside the cafe, waiting for us all to arrive, nursing milky coffee, thumb rolling over the screen of your phone.

Camera is set up on the table, pointing right at the tower, filming. Time is 10.59 and demolition is at noon and it's cold, freezing really, and the wind is making everything difficult: notebook pages fly, hair in my eyes. I sit tight and count the minutes, stretching, ballooning into a perfectly formed half hour, then, later, an hour. I calculate: I haven't heard your voice, haven't seen you, for eight hours, and I think I am falling apart.

One minute until the explosion. Peter is quivering, now,

and my hands are unsteady on the keyboard. A distraction: to think of your lecture, of Ori Gersht, *the moment of destruction, the moment of creation*, the petals flying outwards towards the screen and your voice as you said, 'What is the difference between a painting, and a photograph of a painting?' Kat, Diya, Adam counting down the seconds out loud, twenty-nine, twenty-eight, twenty-seven, lurch of something in my stomach, anticipating the collapse, dropping and squirming and my lungs feel tight, as though the air we're breathing is already thick with dust, and the site around the tower is completely clear, now, nobody is allowed nearby, and there's a loud bang, just as you said there would be, for the birds, and moments later a wisp of birds peels away from the roof and I'm wondering whether that would have been enough, just to film the birds taking off like that, and whether we couldn't have done something afterwards to edit it, to make them look simultaneous – the explosion and the birds – whether *The Ascension of Waderley* couldn't have been, after all, the kind of art that is made *from* fact, rather than the kind that *is* fact, whether a video of an explosion is as good as an explosion, better, even, because it can be rewound in a way that can't be done on YouTube or in life, eighteen, seventeen, sixteen, giving in and looking at your Twitter feed to find a single sentence posted over and over – 'When all lines are broken and no sail appears on the blank horizon, then there remains to the isolated subject in the grip of *taedium vitae* one last thing' – and hundreds of retweets and various comments along the lines of 'Have you been hacked?' but you've posted this sentence before and I remember thinking then that I understood it, but suddenly it seems to mean something else, and there's no delaying it, is there, five, four, as everyone at the table tenses and Peter says, 'Let's do this,' two, one, juts of grey smoke as though the tower has grown arms and is breaking out of itself, and the sway of the upper floors, and there they are, the balloons, astonishing, bobbing, climbing into the air, and everyone is amazed, never really thought it would work, astounded, laughing, strangers pointing and gasping, it's perfect, it's just how we imagined it, the building taking off, drifting upwards, disintegrating in the sky, weightless and speckling the clouds and all above us, now, and I'm so giddy and incredulous and buoyant that I turn to kiss you, because in all the commotion and joy I've forgotten where you aren't.

I'M AFRAID

Mike had been hit by a bus, literally hit by a bus, when he was twenty-two, and had never been the same since. This is what he told Lucy within minutes of meeting her, and Lucy, who was new to the office and sitting at the computer next to Mike's, just had to smile and say, 'Oh my God,' because what else could she say? She had to take his word for it that he wasn't the same, since how would she know, she had only just met him. He looked to be in his forties now.

'I have certain physical idiosyncrasies,' Mike was saying, 'so please don't mind me if I type too loudly.'

'Okay,' said Lucy. 'That's fine.'

She was trying to log in to her email account, which IT had set up that morning with the password 'NewHire305'. Every time she typed it in, the computer said it was wrong.

'Your caps lock is on,' said Mike. He reached out and tapped her keyboard, which felt shocking somehow, as though he had leaned over and pinged her bra. Lucy reminded herself of the physical idiosyncrasies, the bus.

'Thanks,' she said. She logged in. There were three emails in her inbox already, linking to online training modules she needed to complete. There was one about heavy lifting in the workplace, one about professional behaviour in the workplace and one about data protection that did not specify whether or not it was in the workplace. She started with data protection. You should never leave a client's business card facing up on your desk, she learned, because someone walking past might see it, and therefore the client's data could be compromised. Lucy's job title was Internal Corporate Communications Assistant. She was hired to help write emails that would be sent to employees within the company.

'Heavy Lifting in the Workplace' was about how, if you have to pick up a heavy box, you should bend your knees.

'Professional Behaviour in the Workplace' was about how you shouldn't sexually harass anyone, mostly.

Lucy had taken this job because she wanted to prove a point to her ex-boyfriend. After university, she had started something he referred to as her 'side hustle', but since she didn't have any other kind of hustle, Lucy called it her business. She was extremely good at the business, which provided copywriting services for people who were struggling to send difficult emails. The clients told her what the situation was – they wanted their adult child to move out, for example, or had ignored a message from someone for two years but now needed to ask for a favour – and she would write a message for them. Sometimes the situations were really quite sensitive and upsetting, but Lucy had a knack for making them seem manageable. The difficult-email business had started as a kind of joke when she had been wondering what to do with herself after graduation, but it had made an immediate profit.

Soon she was able to do things her friends thought were quite flashy, like live alone and buy a car.

Lucy had imagined she would keep doing this for ever. *Dear Mum and Dad, I'm afraid I have some difficult news to share. After a lot of careful consideration, I have decided I do not want to carry on Dad's carpentry business.* It was rewarding work. It made her feel sort of invincible, like the worries and problems of other people didn't affect her somehow. *There is no easy way to say this, so I'm going to be as honest with you as possible: I'm afraid I cannot go through with this wedding.* She'd been so busy she had to train someone up to work with her, though she always glanced over his writing before she let him send it off. *Something happened to me a long time ago that I've felt unable to share with you until now.* She kept putting up her rates and felt almost appalled when people continued to pay.

In the seventh year of the business, she noticed things getting quieter, but at first hadn't been concerned. She introduced a three-difficult-emails-for-the-price-of-two offer. Fluctuation was surely normal. When things still did not improve, she started a loyalty scheme for repeat customers. She had more than enough in savings to see her through a dry spell, though it was unnerving seeing the balance in the account get lower and lower. She offered loyal clients an option to keep her on retainer. Then, after nearly a whole year of declining interest, she had to make her employee redundant. *Dear Silas,* she wrote to him, *This is a difficult email to have to write.*

Even after that, things continued to decline. Then she happened to hear, on a podcast she enjoyed about quirky things to do with the internet, a story about people using AI to write their difficult emails, and that was it. She knew there was no coming back from it. The business was dead. She threw a small party to mark the occasion and ordered a cake that said 'F U ChatGPT' on it.

'You'll have to figure out what else you're good at,' her then-boyfriend had said. 'There must be something you can do better than a computer.' Her then-boyfriend worked as a financial analyst. She told him he was framing it wrong; she had to find a different outlet for her ability to break bad news. So she had taken this job as an internal corporate communications assistant for the London office of a global company that distributed mining machinery, even though it was an entry-level position that paid a quarter of what she'd made before, even though the job description had not specified that she would be exclusively communicating bad news. It seemed like the sort of company that mostly had bad news for its staff.

A couple of days before starting her new role, she had broken up with her boyfriend because the fact that he had called the business she ran for eight years a side hustle suddenly struck her as unforgiveable. She told him in person, though she'd have preferred to put it in writing.

Mike's job title was Internal Corporate Communications Co-ordinator. What that meant, as far as Lucy could tell, was that he went to meetings with HR where they told him things that needed to be communicated internally to the workforce, and then he told her what those things were so that she could write them down in an email. She then had to send the text of the email to the Internal Corporate Communications Designer, who added some pictures and made the font and layout look the same as all the other emails from the Internal Corporate Communications team.

In Lucy's first week, the things that needed to be communicated internally to the workforce were that people could wear red jumpers in aid of Comic Relief on Friday, that the date of the company picnic was 19 June, and that nominations were now open for the Wondrous Workers awards: colleagues could nominate each other or themselves for the chance to win an extra half day of annual leave. None of this was treated as though it was bad news, though Lucy felt in her bones that it all was, somehow. *This is a very difficult update to have to share,* she typed, *but there will be a company picnic this year.*

Mike looked over at her screen and frowned. 'What are you doing?'

She hit delete repeatedly. 'Just getting warmed up,' she said.

There's no easy way to tell you that nominations for the Wondrous Workers awards are now open.

When she glanced at Mike's screen, he was looking at images of kittens surrounded by pink hearts. The words he'd put into the search engine were 'kitten love heart picture for girlfriend cartoon funny cute'.

'What are you doing?' Lucy said.

Mike maximised a window that had a graph on it. 'Only 38 per cent of recipients opened our last email,' he said, gravely. 'Would you like to get a drink after work?'

It took Lucy a moment to understand that these two sentences were not connected. She chose her words carefully, thinking about professional behaviour in the workplace. She considered the kitten love heart pictures for girlfriend. It was important to seem friendly, she thought, but not too friendly. 'Sure,' she said, 'but I'll need to be home by seven because my boyfriend is cooking dinner.'

'Great,' said Mike. 'I need to be home by six-thirty because my girlfriend is cooking dinner too,' and Lucy thought, *Oh, that girlfriend does not exist, that girlfriend absolutely does not exist,* but she couldn't really judge him as she'd lied first. She should have said a point-blank no to the whole thing, it was obvious now, but that seemed so hostile for her first week. Besides, living alone, which had seemed like a luxury when she had been in a relationship and running her own business and generally doing brilliantly at life now seemed sad and quiet, and she was grateful for something to fill her time. She was also quite interested in learning more about Mike being hit by a bus.

When Mike left his desk, she opened ChatGPT. Black text in the middle of the screen said, 'Where should we begin?' as though they didn't already have a history, ChatGPT and Lucy, as though ChatGPT hadn't already fired some pretty devastating shots her way. *Write an email to company employees telling them they can wear red jumpers for Comic Relief on Friday,* she typed. *Their jobs are something to do with distributing mining machinery, in case that's relevant. Write it like it's really good news.* As soon as she pressed enter and the computer started to reply, filling the screen with its response at an alarming rate, she felt horrible, as though she had somehow cheated on herself. She closed the browser without reading any of it, and then Mike returned with a packet of crisps, sitting down heavily and sighing in a way that made it obvious he wanted her to ask how he was doing.

'What's your boyfriend like?' Mike said, as soon as they'd sat down with their drinks. They were outside in the beer garden, though it wasn't really warm enough; a few other people were out there acting like they weren't cold. Lucy pulled her coat around her and fingered the stem of her wine glass. She wished she'd got something hot. She could have ordered tea. Maybe getting wine made it seem like a date.

'Great,' she said. 'He's a really great guy.' When people had asked her what her ex-boyfriend was like she would say, 'He's a financial analyst.'

'My girlfriend is brilliant too,' said Mike. 'Do you want to see a photo of her?'

'Sure.'

Mike held up his phone, which had a spiderweb of cracks across the glass and a picture on its home screen of a very pretty girl, sort of ludicrously pretty, enormous green eyes and fiery red hair and lips parted precisely to give a glimpse of white teeth and a little dusting of freckles across her pert nose. 'There she is.'

'That's your girlfriend?' said Lucy. She hadn't caught herself before speaking, and was aware her tone was accusatory.

'Yes,' said Mike. He didn't seem to mind the way she'd said it. He took a sip of beer, flipping the phone to face him and smiling at the photo. 'Her name's Cordelia,' he said. He had foam on his top lip. Lucy fought the urge to tell him. She felt quite certain that she disliked Mike; there was something deplorable about giving yourself a fake girlfriend so implausibly beautiful.

Mike said he had met Cordelia on a dating app. There had been instant attraction between them and things had moved very fast. Within a week they were spending hours on the phone together each night, and when they went on their first in-person date – dinner at a Michelin-starred restaurant, he didn't say which – it had been electric. They both knew at once that they were destined to be together. Now they lived together; she was an interior designer with a flourishing business, and she was an amazing cook too.

'How did you meet your boyfriend?'

'At the gym,' Lucy said.

'What's his name?'

'Jason,' she said, which was the name of her ex-boyfriend.

'What does he do?'

The wine had gone straight to Lucy's head and she felt drowsy – not only drowsy but weary, too, of being there in the cold pub garden and talking to this man she hadn't known a week ago, and putting even a moment of unnecessary energy into lying to him.

'Listen, Mike,' she said, 'I don't actually have a boyfriend. I'm sorry. I just made it up in case you were hitting on me.'

'I know,' Mike said. 'You're actually a really bad liar.'

'Oh,' Lucy said, 'right.'

'I should probably come clean with you too,' said Mike,

and Lucy braced. He had committed so hard to his girlfriend story, a photo on his home screen, for God's sake, and now he was going to abandon it, just like that.

'Your girlfriend's not real either?' she said.

Mike frowned. 'No,' he said, 'that's not it at all. Cordelia's definitely real. It's just that I exaggerated a little bit. We've not actually met in person yet. We talk on the phone. Everything else I said is true, it's just that she lives in Sicily and she's looking after her sick mother so she can't visit just yet. I know I shouldn't have lied, but when I tell people that we haven't met yet they seem to take the relationship less seriously, and it's a really serious relationship.'

Lucy sort of laughed then, and reached out to pat him on the arm. She had the feeling she needed to wake him up. 'Mike,' she said. 'Mike. Come on. Your girlfriend isn't real.'

'No,' he said again. 'No, that's not true. I literally speak to her every night.'

When Mike went to the toilet, he left his phone behind on the table. Lucy couldn't believe herself, couldn't actually believe she was doing it, but she reached out and looked at the photo of Cordelia, and then with her own phone she took a photo of the photo. Afterwards, a full-body blush began to creep over her, almost pleasantly warm.

On Friday morning, Lucy realised she didn't own anything red. Three years earlier, when her business was thriving, she'd gone to something called a style studio where she had paid a man quite a lot of money to analyse what colours suited her. There she had learned that she was a soft summer, and afterwards she'd got rid of all the clothes she had that weren't in her personal palette of pale blues and pale pinks and pale greys. She thought she still had a red scarf somewhere but it was nowhere to be found; it must have gone in the cull after all. Every now and then she looked up the man who ran the style studio; his business was still thriving. With hindsight it had been silly, the whole thing – soft summer, the money and getting rid of all those clothes – but at the time she'd felt good about it.

She put her phone and purse and keys in a red tote bag that had come from a bookshop, and that would have to do.

Mike was wearing a red waistcoat and a red tie. He looked baffled when he saw her.

'Where's your red?'

Lucy gestured a little helplessly at her tote bag.

'You were the one who wrote the email,' said Mike. 'You'd think you'd have remembered.'

'Sorry,' said Lucy.

'You would look quite good in red,' Mike said, and Lucy wanted to tell him that he was wrong, actually, she had received professional advice to the contrary, but that would only drag out a conversation that was straying towards something inappropriate, perhaps was already there, since surely commenting on someone's appearance wasn't professional behaviour in the workplace. But then, Mike had been hit by a bus.

'How's Cordelia?' she asked.

Mike's face lit up and Lucy felt kind of fascinated to see it happen, the way his features seemed to rearrange themselves into something calmer and clearer and honestly quite pleasant at the mention of her name.

'Really bad,' said Mike. 'Her mum's really ill. She thinks it might be, you know, endgame territory.'

Lucy caught herself thinking about Cordelia at times when she had no business thinking about Cordelia. On Saturday, after her first full week at work, she felt restless and bored, which wasn't something she was used to feeling; she thought of herself as both busy and easily amused. Perhaps this was a consequence of not having the business any more, of suddenly being somebody's employee. It made your free time feel so pressured and so empty. She was supposed to be enjoying her weekend! And because she was supposed to be enjoying it, that too felt like an obligation dictated by her employer. She made coffee with the proper coffee maker, which on the weekday mornings she hadn't had time to use. She ate toast slowly, scrolling the news. And then she ended up pondering Mike's fake girlfriend and staring at the photo of the photo of Cordelia on Mike's phone, those enormous green eyes peering out through the network of cracks on Mike's screen.

Lucy opened her laptop and searched 'fake girlfriend red hair green eyes freckles', but all that came up were the faces of other fake girlfriends on the internet. She searched 'AI image of pretty redhead girl green eyes' and found lots of AI images of pretty redheads that weren't Cordelia. It was impossible, absolutely impossible, that Cordelia was a real person, and Lucy was taken aback that this wasn't immediately provable.

She texted a friend asking if he was free for lunch, and

then another friend, and then a tier-two friend because the first two were busy. They had entered into a phase of their lives where social engagements needed to be planned weeks in advance; negotiations were long and detailed – *Can't do the 14th, is the 19th any good? Can't do the 19th, how's 8 a.m. on the 26th? Ah, I've got yoga at 8 that day . . .* – and seemed to be a sort of showing off, if Lucy was honest, about how busy and loved and effective they all were. She was as guilty of it as the rest of them, except for now, when she was immediately available and troubled by it. Nobody was free.

She thumbed back through her message history until she got to Jason. The last time they had texted was five weeks earlier, when she had said, *I left your stuff with Natalie,* and he had said, *Okay thanks,* and she had, for some reason, also written, *Okay thanks,* and then he had written, *I really don't see why we have to do this, I thought we were really good, I thought you were really happy, I don't understand what I did wrong.*

It struck her now, looking back over this exchange, that it was cruel not to have replied. She had just left all of that sadness hanging on the left-hand side of the screen, as though Jason was awful when he wasn't, that wasn't the point. They had gone over and over it all, the reasons for the break-up; she had already answered all his questions several times. But still, it felt unnecessary to have said nothing at all.

Hey Jason, she texted. *What are you up to today?*

He wrote back immediately. *Not much you?*

Just checking you're doing okay, she wrote and immediately dots rippled on Jason's side of the screen. He was always so horrifically fast at replying. She flipped her phone face down on the counter and drank her coffee too quickly. It had been wrong not to reply at the time, but it was wrong, too, to stir it up again weeks later.

She was enjoying a leisurely Saturday. And somewhere, in some unreachable place, the person who was pretending to be Cordelia was having a Saturday, too.

'what is the fake girlfriend scam' she searched.

'what to do if your friend is being scammed online' she searched.

'what to do if your colleague is being scammed online' she searched, because Mike wasn't a friend; she didn't really know him at all.

On Monday, the first thing Mike said was, 'You'll be busy next week, Lucy.'

'Oh,' she said, 'will I?'

'Yes,' he said, 'bit of an in-at-the-deep-end situation for you, covering for me so soon into the job.'

Oh,' she said. 'Right.'

'But it can't be helped,' he said. 'I've had to take annual leave. Urgently.'

Lucy began counting in her head, and Mike had said 'Cordelia' before she even reached three.

'Cordelia needs me. I'm flying to Palermo.'

'What happened?' said Lucy, though she could imagine what had happened because she'd spent most of her weekend reading accounts of online romance scams, which were always more or less the same. Cordelia's sick mother would have taken a turn for the worse, and the hospital would suddenly have produced a bill that the family couldn't afford to pay, and unless they somehow found the money her mother would die, and so she would have asked Mike to send it to her. And Mike had probably sent her the money, but not only that: he had probably also decided that he needed to fly out to Sicily to be with his girlfriend at this difficult time, despite her protestations that he shouldn't. 'Is it Cordelia's mother?'

'Yes,' said Mike.

'Sorry to hear that,' said Lucy, and idly typed in a search about the Italian healthcare system, wondering whether it was even plausible that someone in Sicily would have a medical bill. *Italy's healthcare system, the Servizio Sanitario Nazionale (SSN), is a universal, tax-funded public system providing comprehensive health services to all citizens and legal residents.*

Lucy's phone buzzed and before she had a chance to look at it, Mike leaned over and said, 'Jason has texted you.'

'Thanks.' Lucy slid the phone closer to her.

'Isn't that the name of your fake boyfriend?' said Mike.

Hey, are you busy? Jason had texted.

'Did you give your fake boyfriend the name of someone you know?' said Mike.

Passing by your new office and wanted to drop something off for you, said Jason.

'Is it someone you wish was your actual boyfriend?' said Mike.

When Lucy got to the ground-floor reception area, Jason was sitting in one of the low chairs by the revolving doors. There was a bunch of flowers on the coffee table by his knees. He was bouncing his leg up and down.

'Why aren't you at work?' said Lucy, and in the second between asking the question and hearing the answer, entertained a fantasy about Jason being laid off because AI could do his job faster and more reliably than he could.

'I took some time off,' he said.

The flowers on the table were really very nice; Jason had always been good at things like that. He understood that carnations didn't really count, for some reason; he understood that it was too obvious to do red roses. There were irises in the bouquet and some sort of frothy, cream-coloured blossom.

'What is it this company actually does?' he said, eyeing the logo over the reception area.

'Something to do with distributing machinery,' said Lucy. 'But I'm not involved with that. Why are you here?'

'I just thought you should know,' Jason said, and then looked over his shoulder as though he was worried he'd been followed, 'that I'm thinking of you.'

'Okay,' said Lucy.

Jason pushed the bouquet across the table. It had a strong smell, almost peppery.

'I was really glad you texted on Saturday,' he said. 'It was very reassuring.'

They had been a couple all those years and Lucy couldn't think of a time Jason had ever previously used the word reassuring, had ever needed reassurance about anything. When they'd first got together – they'd met in the first week of university, living on the same corridor; had been locked out of their accommodation after a smoke alarm went off at

3 a.m. and bonded over the experience – it was a word Lucy might have used to describe him. He broadly behaved the way you would expect a person to behave, and that was reassuring; she'd always found it reassuring. He always did what he said he would do. He said he'd call her when he got back from his night out. He said he'd love to meet her parents. He said he would get an economics degree and a good summer internship and then move to London.

There were other people at their university, people who studied business or economics or possibly maths, who made it a point of pride that things came easily to them. They would go through a big performance of not trying hard; they wanted it to be known that good things just seemed to fall into their laps: good marks on their coursework, work experience, then, later, jobs in the city that had something to do with moving money around. Jason wasn't like that, and Lucy had appreciated it. Jason said he would try hard and then did try hard, and that had counted for a lot, that he was willing to be seen to try.

Jason said he would propose the summer before they both turned thirty, and that had felt reassuring, until it had begun to feel like a threat.

'Okay,' said Jason, nodding. 'That was it, really. I'm thinking of you.' And then he got up and left, looking over his shoulder again.

Lucy felt a little dazed as she carried the flowers up in the lift. She couldn't tell whether the scent was pleasant or not; there was perhaps a slight edge of rot to it, especially when the air was so close and still around her. Jason had looked incredibly nervous, as though he was committing a huge transgression, and she hadn't known how to react. It was apparent that after all she should have sent a clearer message, made it obvious that the break-up still stood, even if she had texted to check in on him; there was no way to interpret 'I'm thinking of you' accompanied by flowers as anything other than a bid for reconciliation, was there? There was no other way to interpret his use of the word 'reassuring'.

She drifted past banks of desks and noticed for the first time how empty it was in the office, the unused chairs and blank screens of the people working from home and how even the employees who showed up barely spoke, how quiet it was. And then there was Mike, who never worked from home, who believed that the internal communications team should internally communicate in person, five days a week. And there was Mike's voice carrying all the way from the corner where the internal communications team sat, saying, 'And Lucy will handle that while I'm away,' in the direction of the office manager.

'What will I handle?' She sat down at her computer.

'What are those?' said Mike.

'Flowers.' She set them in a chipped blue mug she'd taken from the kitchen, and tipped in water from her flask.

'Flowers from Jason,' said Mike, as though he was correcting her.

As the week went on, Mike continued to add items to the list of things Lucy would cover while he was away, none of which appeared to require more than a few minutes of her time, and the flowers from Jason began to smell increasingly sour, and Lucy became more and more concerned about Mike's trip to Sicily. It was just that he was so excited, so utterly unprepared for the reality of what awaited him, and she had also begun to wonder about the relevance of Sicily, which seemed unusual as the setting for this kind of scam and maybe indicated something to do with the mafia. It sounded far-fetched and she hadn't said it out loud to anybody, but she had started to imagine the worst. (And what was the worst, exactly? Some sort of kidnapping scenario?) Mike didn't seem to have friends who could help him. He never spoke of anyone in his life apart from Cordelia. And then, on the Friday afternoon, Lucy returned from lunch to find Mike emptying a little sachet of flower food into her chipped blue mug, and she realised perhaps it was her: she was the friend, she was the one who was supposed to protect him.

'Have you ever actually *seen* Cordelia?' she asked.

'I told you, we've never met.'

'But have you ever done a FaceTime or video call or anything like that?'

'Oh,' said Mike. 'No. I asked her a few times, but she was always so tired from work.'

'Too tired to have a face?'

Mike looked wounded. 'I think she wanted a chance to do her make-up nicely before anything like that,' he said. 'Which is understandable.'

'I don't think you should go to Sicily,' Lucy said. 'You must know, you have to know, that Cordelia is not a real person, Mike. She's not a real person.'

Mike looked at her blankly. 'You're mistaken, I'm afraid.' And then, as though the phrase was stuck in his head, he repeated it. 'I'm afraid. I'm afraid I *am* going to Sicily.'

So that was it. She had tried. And on Saturday she found she was checking the time and thinking about Mike, about where he would have got to on his journey. It was 11 a.m., which meant he'd have arrived at the airport, and perhaps was making his way through security. It was midday, so he was probably at the gate. The flight departed at 12.30 p.m., which she knew because he had written it down on a piece of paper and stuck it to his desk in the hope, she supposed, that people passing by would notice and maybe ask him about it. It was 1 p.m., so Mike was in the air. It was 2 p.m., so Mike was still in the air.

She went to the gym and then the supermarket and later on she had dinner plans with friends, so it wasn't like she wasn't busy, it wasn't like she didn't have a full life. She had left her phone at home, which felt sort of radical and quite nice, freeing, but it meant that when she got back to the flat, the burlap handle of the shopping bag digging hard into her forearm, Jason was there sitting with his back to her front door, and she'd had no warning.

As soon as she got inside, having awkwardly invited him to follow her, she checked the time. It was 4.30 p.m., which meant it was 5.30 p.m. in Sicily and Mike would be on the ground, somewhere, would have made it through baggage reclaim and be waiting at arrivals, would have been waiting there for a little while by then, would possibly that very moment be beginning to doubt whether Cordelia was really coming.

Jason made himself tea, filling the kettle as though the water in the tap was his water, reaching easily up to the cupboard where the mugs were. Then he sat on the side of the sofa he always sat on. There was something robotic about him, Lucy thought, the way he moved the same way all the time.

'Why are you here, Jason?' she asked. 'What do you want?'

'Where are your flowers?'

'What flowers?'

'The ones I gave you.' He bent his head towards his tea, though it was surely too hot to drink, and then straightened again without drinking.

'Oh,' said Lucy. 'They're at work.'

Jason looked baffled but didn't say anything, leaning again towards and then away from his mug. He had redeeming features, Lucy thought. The things she had thought were good about him when they were together were still good, the solidness of him, the way he tried hard at everything. But oh, she had not been missing him, she had not been missing him at all, even when she had been bored and wrong-footed by the rhythm of her new life and had missed having something to do, even when it was she who had texted him first, she had not been missing him. He had called her business a side hustle.

She checked the time again. Mike would have been waiting for Cordelia for around forty minutes.

'I'm not sure why you're here,' she said to Jason. 'We broke up and I don't want to be with you any more.'

Jason looked astonished, as though she had hit him; he jolted and a small wave of tea sluiced onto the arm of the sofa. 'What do you mean?' he said.

'We broke up.'

'But then why did you take the flowers?' Jason said, still looked flabbergasted, genuinely confused, not even angry, just completely lost. 'Why did you text me about my day?'

There was a sort of hot smell to the arrivals hall of Palermo airport, like the smell after a summer rain shower in London, Mike thought, except there was no rain; it seemed arid, almost. There was a little cafe, and after a while he thought he might as well go over and order a coffee, practise his Italian, which he'd been working on since first meeting Cordelia. When he reached the front of the queue and opened his mouth, however, he found he could remember nothing; the man at the counter smiled and seemed in no hurry, he could take his time, but in the end he ordered an espresso since that was at least the same in both languages. He took the little paper cup back to the spot where he'd been waiting for Cordelia, because it had the best vantage over every door to the building, so he'd be sure to see her as soon as she arrived. The espresso was too strong and too bitter; he only really liked coffee when there was lots of milk in it, but it helped to have something to hold.

Ciao, Cordelia, he would say when she arrived. He wouldn't mess that up. *Ciao, Cordelia, mia bellissima ragazza.* He'd written this phrase on a piece of paper that was at that very moment folded in his pocket, so he could refer to it if needed.

She'd confirmed she'd be there at the airport. They had spoken that morning, and she had sounded as chirpy as ever, excited to see him; she didn't have a car, she said, but she would take the bus to get to him and he shouldn't worry about how long that would take her or whether she would be safe as a single woman travelling alone or anything like that. He had sent over her cab fare. Her mother was still very ill, she said, and they were considering paying for an in-home nurse, though they couldn't really afford one. It was possible she had saved the cab fare towards paying for the nurse and taken the bus instead, which would explain the lateness and would be entirely understandable, completely forgivable considering the situation.

It was also possible, he knew, that Cordelia wasn't coming. He had watched a documentary about exactly this kind of thing, and the men in the film had seemed sort of familiar, like he had something in common with them, maybe just that they were lonely, but they hadn't seemed like losers. Perhaps Cordelia wasn't coming and perhaps none of what she had told him was true and perhaps the pretty girl in the picture that was saved to his home screen wasn't even the girl he had been talking to. Perhaps the girl he had been talking to wasn't even a girl, he knew that was possible too. It wasn't like he was naive; he had several alter egos online, which he used to post opinions he wasn't sure he really held, and he sometimes even argued with himself in the comments.

Outside the airport, it looked extremely hot. The sunlight was a very dark gold, and the strip of pavement it fell on was also gold. There were taxis and occasional buses that pulled in and made his heart race, then pulled away again without depositing Cordelia. He tried calling her again but it wouldn't connect. Then his phone buzzed and it was a text, at last, a message, but it was just from the new girl at work. *How are you doing?*

He took a selfie holding up his espresso in the manner of someone who enjoyed espresso and sent it to her.

How are you doing? Lucy wrote again. *Is Cordelia there?*

Mike had been a bit baffled by Lucy's commitment to disproving Cordelia's existence. It seemed unnecessary and also awkward. He wasn't used to other people making things awkward for him, it was usually the other way round. He thought of himself like that: an odd and awkward guy. He knew this about himself, accepted it even. For a while he had even tried introducing himself that way: *Hi, I'm Mike, I'm afraid I'm a bit of an odd guy.* It hadn't gone over the way he'd hoped. It set people on edge, even more than usual, and he'd felt angry then, almost wished he was odder, because if he was odder people would probably make allowances, might even be kind, rather than tuning him out or laughing at him in the staff kitchen. Once, he had walked back to his desk after a meeting to find a colleague sitting at his desk, doing an impression of him typing. It was immediately recognisable. He knew he typed too loudly. Wished he didn't. Couldn't help it.

He could lie to Lucy, he thought, and say that he and Cordelia were at that very moment engaged in a passionate embrace on a picturesque beach but instead he wrote, *She's on her way. Bus delayed.*

What are you going to do? wrote Lucy, which struck him as a non sequitur. Still, it was a good question. Because what was he going to do, now he was here in Palermo and disliked espresso and Cordelia wasn't there, which meant, really, that

Cordelia wasn't coming, which in turn meant, didn't it, that Cordelia wasn't real and he was just another lonely guy who'd fallen for a dumb trick like those lonely guys in that documentary, and on top of that he was odd, an odd and lonely guy?

He was panicking. He knew he was, and that was never a good thing, panicking; it made you lose your head and do unpredictable things.

A bus pulled up to the pavement outside and he held his breath, scanning the heads of the people disembarking for Cordelia's auburn hair, and when she wasn't there he found that he was running towards it, running so fast he spilled the espresso, and was flying through the automatic doors into a wall of heat, so thick and heavy all around him he almost cried out, and then he was leaping up the stairs of the bus and waving money towards the driver and saying – at last his Italian was kicking in! – '*Un biglietto per dove stai andando, per favore!*' The engine rumbled as he stumbled towards a seat and then sat and let his head fall against the juddering window, and he was in Sicily, there it was, its strange smells and its heat and its unfamiliar sounds and nobody there who knew who he was or cared about him, and generally in the world there were not people who cared about him, not really, not in the way that people seemed to care about each other, and as the bus moved away from the airport the view from the window seemed to get stranger and stranger and he did not know where he was going and of course Cordelia was not real, he had known that all along.

*

It had been quite difficult for Lucy to corral Jason out of her flat, and afterwards she felt drained in a way that reminded her of how she would feel after swimming lessons as a child. She slumped on the sofa, on what had once been Jason's side, and struggled to keep her eyes open. There had been a point during their stand-off when Jason had locked himself in the bathroom and Lucy had threatened to call the police, but what she had actually done was text Mike to ask if he was all right, and he had sent her a photo of himself holding a coffee. And then Jason had shuffled out of the bathroom of his own accord because she'd gone quiet on him and he was feeling ignored.

She forced her eyes open in order to write a formal dismissal to Jason: *I understand the distress this is causing you, but feel it's important to put this in writing.* And then she texted Mike again, because he'd been at the airport for hours at that point and seemed no closer to realising what was really going on. *How are you doing?*

She only knew she'd fallen asleep because her phone ringing woke her up, and she hadn't even really registered who it was when she answered. Mike's voice sounded slightly electronic; the line was bad. 'Hello?' he was saying. 'Hello?'

'Mike,' she said. 'Are you all right?'

'Fine,' he said. 'Absolutely fine. On a bus.'

'Where are you going?' she asked. 'Is Cordelia with you?'

'I need to come clean about something, Lucy,' Mike said.

Lucy felt a rush of horror, a kind of wave of empathy that made her want to cry. She felt almost unbearably sorry for Mike, who didn't have anything in his life, really had nothing.

'It's okay,' she said. 'You don't need to tell me. I know. I already know.'

'No,' Mike said, 'oh, no, it's not what you think. Are you there? I said it's not what you think.'

'Cordelia,' Lucy said, but Mike was still speaking.

'I need to be honest with you about something I lied about. I wasn't ever actually hit by a bus. It's just something I made up so you didn't think I was strange for no reason.'

'Where are you going?' Lucy asked.

'I don't know,' said Mike.

Lucy tried to tell him again about Cordelia, about Cordelia not being real, but he was talking and didn't seem to hear her, was saying something about the bus, the bus he was on or the bus that hadn't really hit him, she wasn't sure which, the line was bad, so in the end she cut the call. Her flat was very quiet. Her sofa was very still. She thought about Mike on the bus. She thought about the way Mike had said, when he first told her his plans, 'I'm afraid. I'm afraid I *am* going to Sicily,' and she found herself typing again, the sentences familiar, reassuring: *There's no easy way to say what I'm about to say, and I realise you have been resistant to hearing this in the past. It's important for your well-being that I tell you this now.* But before she pressed send, Mike texted her: no words, just a photo of a view of a roadside though a window, patchy grass and a stone wall that looked old and a city in the distance, yellow and sunlit, and you could see, too, the reflection of Mike's face in the glass, the curve of his jaw and shadow under his nose and it looked, it really did look, like he was smiling.

The Reading

What you must bear in mind throughout everything that follows is that while it was going on, I was suffering an extreme allergic reaction to a yoga mat. When I tell you about the wedding and my friend Amelia, and Henry, and the reading, you should keep the allergic reaction at the forefront of your mind. It was certainly at the front, or near enough, of mine. The rash was mostly on my palms and the itching was constant, bad enough to keep me up at night. My waking life was preoccupied with the question of whether scratching each hand with the other would make it better or worse.

I was thinking about scratching – about the urge to do something that hurts, about how my grandmother had told me that it doesn't help the itching, it just supplants the original discomfort with one more urgent – up to and including the moment I first saw Henry at the wedding. I'd parked down the road and walked uphill to the church; I was slightly out of breath and the cold air had aggravated my skin. He was standing with his groomsmen at the door, wide-smiling and laughing that gooseish, good-natured laugh of his, greeting guests as they filed past, and I realised he was the only person I've ever truly loathed.

I hung back by the gravestones and scratched my left palm

with the ring finger of my right hand. The relief was ecstatic and temporary.

Henry looked up, saw me, and waved.

'Kate! So glad you could make it,' he called out, and his smile was just flawless, fixed, totally convincing.

I shuffled out from among the headstones.

'All set for the reading?' he said, and reached forwards to shake my hand.

I'd taken an overnight flight from Austin to London, landed at Heathrow mid-morning and hired a car for the three-hour drive to the wedding. The vehicle smelled chemical and sterile, and the whole way I was in agony holding the steering wheel. I imagined whatever cleaning fluid the car rental company had used was seeping into my sores.

It wasn't just my palms that were affected. My feet, arms and a sliver of my midriff – any part of my skin that had come into contact with the mat – were painful, too, though not as bad. In the hour after the yoga class, my palms had prickled and turned red. By the following morning, they had developed into lava fields of blisters. They looked like bubble wrap, pustules pushing into and against each other. Touching anything caused me acute pain.

I tried to steer with my fingertips. I'd only moved to Austin a few months previously but I'd already adjusted to driving on the right; whenever my attention wandered from the task at hand, I could feel the car drifting towards the other side of the road.

*

Amelia had first mentioned the reading on a FaceTime call with a bad connection; my video kept freezing, catching my expression without fail at its most grotesque, chins and grimaces, a monstrous dollop of tongue protruding. My grandmother's bungalow didn't have internet so I was in the Starbucks down the road, air-conditioned to the point of refrigeration and wearing a hoodie though it was forty degrees outside.

'What time is it there?' she asked. It was mid-afternoon in Austin and I had left my grandmother in her armchair shouting insults at the talking heads on CNN. Amelia was six hours ahead in London and was getting ready to go to a party, squinting into her screen as she applied mascara. She always pulled this pained, elongated face when she put make-up on. It made her look horsey, but also it reminded me of her at thirteen, daubing her eyelids with electric-blue eyeshadow that had come free with a magazine.

'Listen,' she said, 'about the wedding. It's really important to me that you're there,' which is how I knew there had been a conversation between her and Henry about the possibility that I should not be there.

Then she said, 'I want you to give a reading,' which was how I knew that what I was being offered was the result of intense negotiations between her and Henry. It had been understood between her and me for years, long before she met Henry and got engaged, that I'd be one of her bridesmaids. 'I want you to give a reading' meant: this is the best you're going to get, considering the circumstances.

The reading she asked me to give was from Ecclesiastes 4.

It began, 'So I returned, and considered all the oppressions that are done under the sun,' which I found an odd starting point for a wedding, and it got odder, because there was a bit about how it was better to be dead than alive because of all the awful things that people do to each other. Once it got going it was clearer what it was getting at, which was a whole thing about togetherness, about how two are stronger than one. At the end it said, 'Better is a poor and a wise child than an old and foolish king,' but I was supposed to stop reading before that line.

'Listen,' Amelia said. 'I've got to go.'

Henry had appeared on the screen behind her, adjusting his tie and saying something inaudible.

'I'm making us late,' she said.

'Hi, Henry,' I said, but Amelia was already blowing kisses and saying, 'Bye bye bye bye bye bye bye,' and then the screen went black.

So I returned, and considered all the oppressions that are done under the sun.

There was something exposing about being back in England. I felt people could read me too easily. In Texas, I was outside of things, irrelevant and un-implicated. I'd moved there to take care of my dying grandmother, who lived in a bungalow with three cats and an uncountable number of chickens shuffling around outside in the yard. It was hot, and quiet, and when people heard my accent they thought of things that were nothing to do with me, like the royal family, or tea. The minute I landed in London I felt like an open book, as though anyone could tell, just by looking at my face and haircut and clothes and the way I walked, what sort of person I was. When I spoke, even just to the man at the car-hire booth or the listless teenaged barista at the service station, where I stopped to buy two large black coffees, they knew even more: how much money my parents had, what part of the country I'd grown up in, what sort of school I'd gone to. None of which mattered, exactly, but it contributed to the feeling I had that the whole thing was a mistake. I felt unpeeled.

My bank texted me to confirm the service-station coffee transaction was really mine.

If I hadn't said yes to doing the reading, I might have kept on driving past the church.

Henry's hand extended towards mine, and behind him the doorway to the church was yawning.

'Hi, Henry,' I said, and instead of shaking his hand, I spread my palms out apologetically. 'I'm afraid I can't—' I said. 'My hands—' I said. I used one to gesture towards the other. And then I said, 'Congratulations.'

Henry's eyes lowered to my palms, and for a fraction of a second his smile faltered. Even his public-schoolboy charm, which seemed to me to function like a kind of body armour, couldn't completely withstand the sight of the rash.

'Great to see you, Kate,' he said, and then, again, 'All set for the reading?'

I patted my pocket, where I'd tucked the folded piece of paper with Ecclesiastes 4 on it.

'Amelia's taking pictures with the bridesmaids in the vicarage,' he said. 'She said to tell you to go round.'

He pointed towards a path, and I smiled and said congratulations again in a way I thought was definite and conciliatory, and as I walked off I knew he was watching me. I felt as though I couldn't remember how to walk like a person.

Amelia's mother answered the vicarage door, wearing a yellow dress, and looking flustered. She said, 'I'm *so* pleased you're here,' in a way that suggested she knew about everything. 'The girls are in the back.' She waved me down the hallway. I could hear their voices, sharp as car alarms.

The bridesmaids were Henry's sisters and two women who had been to law school with Amelia. I had met the law-school friends several times at birthday parties over the years, but they never seemed to remember having been introduced before; they always said how nice it was to meet me.

They were all wearing blue silk dresses and they looked beautiful, really beautiful, in a way I simply would not have, if I'd been one of them. It was a sort of moneyed beauty that they had, a very specific kind of glossy hair that held curls and could support a crown of dusky pink roses, mouths that opened into perfect semicircles when they threw their heads back to laugh for the camera. Teeth. They all had such rich-looking teeth, and so many of them.

I hovered on the threshold, not wanting to ruin any photographs. The photographer was asking them to pretend to be doing their make-up, though it was clear a professional had already done it for them. The room smelled of my friend's perfume and champagne.

Amelia was sitting in front of a mirror in her white dress, very still, watching them all.

'Hi,' I said, once I felt I'd been there for an uncomfortable amount of time.

Nobody noticed.

I said, 'Hi,' again, and then everyone turned around.

When we were fifteen, Amelia told me she thought she might be gay. I had a boyfriend at the time – I always had a boyfriend; at no point between the ages of fourteen and thirty-four did I not have a boyfriend, two decades of boyfriends, and when I think of them now, I picture them all lined up neatly shoulder to shoulder, the boyfriends, affable and earnest and polite to my parents and, ultimately, defunct – and I told her she probably wasn't. Gayness seemed improbable then, in the age of Section 28 and *Will and Grace* and my dad calling every short-haired woman he met either Thelma or Louise, though he hadn't seen the film and didn't know it wasn't actually about lesbians. Being gay was something embarrassing that other people did, and certainly not anybody we knew, and also I had the phrase 'just a phase' in my head, which was reassuring.

'You just haven't met your person yet,' I said, by which I meant she hadn't met the right boy from the boys' school down the road. We idolised those boys because they were dropped off in nice cars and played rugby and wore real aftershave, while the boys at our own school were ordinary and wore Lynx Africa. Amelia in that moment looked a little relieved, and I felt I had done a good thing, been a good friend, by saying what I'd said.

We were sitting on the floor of her bedroom, taking a

magazine quiz called 'What Kind of Girlfriend Are You?' You had to tally how many of your answers were A, B or C, and at the end it told you what kind of girlfriend you were. My answers were mostly A, which meant I was a 'serious girlfriend', and hers were mostly C, which meant she was a 'flirty girlfriend', even though she'd never been any kind of girlfriend at all.

'How do I meet my person, though?' she said. 'What if I never meet my person?' These seemed like *the* questions we had to answer in our lives: who our person might be, how to find them, how to know we'd found them when we found them, more urgent than anything to do with jobs or exams or university or friends or truly anything at all. It was the great unknown of our existence.

Twenty years later, I told Amelia I was gay and she told me she'd always known I was.

The fool foldeth his hands together, and eateth his own flesh.

I was surprised by how happy I was in Austin, where I'd arrived knowing nobody except an ailing 90-year-old and where it was so hot that breathing the air outside at midday felt like drowning. I liked hearing my grandmother's snores when I went into her room in the morning wondering whether she'd died overnight. I liked sitting with her under her wind chimes, watching the chickens. I liked the way she talked to and about me, the way nobody ever had before – 'Look,' she said, 'you're a dyke, Kate, and that's fine' – and the food we ate together: microwave burritos, 'salads' from the store in plastic boxes that contained pasta, cheese, cubes of ham, croutons and a single, intrepid lettuce leaf. I liked going to the supermarket, where there were always free samples and you could buy wine to drink in a paper cup as you went round.

At first Amelia and I pretended nothing had changed. We texted each other good morning and goodnight, though our mornings and nights weren't at the same time any more. She sent me a photograph of what she wanted her new hair to look like. I sent her pictures of the chickens. She sent me links to videos of people squeezing their own blackheads, which she claimed to find relaxing. Sometimes I'd text *How's Henry?* to be the bigger person, and she'd say he was fine or that he had a cold or whatever. But over time, I found that I was having to remind myself to respond to her. Once, I opened our messages and realised I'd left a *How's your day going?* unanswered, just floating there for four days. My replies always seemed to start, *So sorry for the slow reply!*

I started seeing someone from a dating app, a girl called Tati whom I liked a lot, and my grandmother seemed to like too. When I saw a cute dog in the park or had a weird dream or when my grandmother said she thought Ted Cruz was 'regrettably hot', it was Tati I texted, not my friend.

The craziest thing happened at work today, Amelia texted.

Shall we FaceTime at the weekend? Amelia texted.

I just finished reading this, Amelia texted, and sent a photo of the cover of the book. *I think you'd really like it.*

So sorry for the slow reply! I texted.

Shall we FaceTime at the weekend? Amelia texted.

*

When Amelia first told me about Henry, what she mentioned before anything else was that he loved baking, as though this was not only the central element of his personality but the most desirable. They had made brownies together as a first date. Then he made her a coffee and walnut cake and dropped it off at her desk. For a colleague's retirement party, Henry made strawberry cupcakes, even though the company had ordered catering. For a charity coffee morning, Henry made a lemon poppy-seed loaf.

Their second date was to an exhibition of Winston Churchill's wartime letters, because Henry loved Winston Churchill.

Gradually the portrait she gave me rounded out a little: the car he drove and the fact he drove at all when he lived just off Sloane Square, the school he'd been to, what his family was like, his opinions. I mean, my God: his endless, awful opinions.

When I described Henry to my grandmother I said: there is a painting in his family home so racist that when they opened the gallery to the public, they had to put a little plaque underneath it explaining.

'Oh my God,' Amelia said, 'you're here.'

She looked pale and a little too thin. Her wedding make-up was sitting uneasily on top of her skin. She got up to hug me, moving stiffly in her white dress, and the hug was wonderful. She smelled of herself. Her hair was so full of hairspray that it audibly crunched between our torsos, and she made a joke about being flammable. The shape of her shoulders and chest was familiar and I didn't have to worry about what to do with my own body in order to hold her. It seemed suddenly extraordinary that we had been so far apart.

When we stepped back from each other she saw my hands, and I knew she'd be delighted by them, because she was fascinated by that kind of thing, like the blackhead videos.

'Oh my God,' she said. 'What happened?'

She held up my palm, like a fortune-teller, and I explained about the yoga mat. We both stared at the blisters, the raw-red-raised skin like a crumpet or coral. All the lines were obscured.

'Have you heard of trypophobia?' she asked. 'If you had trypophobia, you'd be really freaked out right now.'

'I *am* really freaked out right now,' I said, though I was not freaked out by the fact of the holes, I was freaked out by the fact of the holes being in my hands.

'Oh my God, I can't stop looking at it,' said Amelia. And then I became aware that the bridesmaids had gone quiet and the photographer had stopped taking pictures and everyone was staring at us, expectantly.

My friend said, 'This is my best friend, Kate,' and I felt the lovely, confused eyes of the bridesmaids take me in: late, dishevelled, covered in holes. I'd changed into my wedding clothes in the loos at the service station, using baby wipes to freshen up and running my fingers through my hair. In the mirrors above the sinks I'd looked okay, but suddenly I knew that I didn't – or at least I did not look okay to these shiny, rosy people who were bridesmaids when I wasn't.

'I'm giving a reading,' I said.

'How lovely,' said one of Henry's sisters.

'It's so nice to finally meet you,' said one of the law-school friends.

Two are better than one, For if they fall, the one will lift up his fellow.

One of the things I liked about Texas was how unabashed its weather was, how when it was hot it was truly, disgustingly hot, and how when it rained it was like someone had flushed a toilet over the whole city, and how sometimes there were tornadoes and I had to chase all the chickens down into the cellar.

'I think there's something unhealthy about living in a place where the weather can't kill you,' my grandmother said, when I asked if she missed living in England.

'Henry says that if global warming is making the earth hotter, why is it so damn cold in London?' Amelia once said.

I met Henry early on in their relationship, before his awfulness really blossomed. We were in a pub garden on a sunny day and everything seemed set up to be pleasant: it was one of the first warm days of the year, when everyone in London is briefly unbuttoned and friendly. I was predisposed to like Henry because Amelia liked him, and because she hadn't yet told me anything that made me dislike him. He was sitting outside and had ordered a pitcher of Pimm's for everyone to share, and stood up when I arrived to kiss me on the cheek. He had the kind of voice that sounded like it should belong to a ginger cat. Within about twenty minutes of meeting me, he'd told me that straight white men were the most disadvantaged demographic in society.

Amelia's mother looked into the room where I was standing among the bridesmaids and said we should think about getting going and I could have kissed her. Instead I kissed Amelia on the cheek, as casually as I could, the way a best friend would, surely, in that situation, and said I should go and find my spot in the church, and good luck, and I'd see her there. I made for the exit and felt that if I could just get out of the bridesmaids' sight, I'd feel all right again.

'Wait,' Amelia said, and I waited. She came to the doorway. She bent her head near to mine, as though she was about to tell me a secret, and my heart started beating very fast. She was close enough that I could see where her lip liner exceeded the boundary of her lips.

'Are you okay?' I asked.

'I don't want it to be awkward,' she said, 'that you're not a bridesmaid. I just didn't want you to feel awkward. I didn't want you to feel awkward because you're the only gay person at the wedding.'

Woe to him that is alone when he falleth; for he hath not another to help him up.

About four months into her relationship with Henry, Amelia started coming to my flat in the middle of the night – midnight, 2 a.m., 4 a.m. – letting herself in with the key I once gave her so she could water my plants while I was away, and crawling into bed next to me. Henry had been texting someone from work on his personal phone and wouldn't show her the messages. Or: Henry had gone out to get them breakfast and she had followed him and caught him calling somebody, making plans to meet up. When confronted, he'd claimed he was just talking to his cousin. Or: Henry had left his phone unlocked while he showered and she had read all his texts and all her suspicions were confirmed; he'd been meeting up with this girl from work and they had even gone to Henry's favourite restaurant together.

Henry said she was crazy and had misunderstood, but she had not misunderstood.

'Leave him,' I would say. 'He's terrible.'

And she'd say yes, yes she would leave him, and I'd plan activities to keep her distracted, like going to art galleries, or to Brighton on the train. Once, we went to the pool and swam lengths in silence, and every time we passed each other in our lane, me swimming one way and she the other, our toes would touch and I'd feel like I should have something to say to her, something witty or diverting or consoling. We swam in silence for forty-five minutes and when we got out I felt tired, that weighed-down, chlorinated, bottomless kind of tiredness, and went to the toilets to cry, though I didn't know why.

I rehearsed with her, over and over, the things she needed to say to Henry about respect, and decency, and honesty, and she was leaving him because, and so on. She'd go into those conversations like a prizefighter, determined, focused, and I was behind her hyping her up, practically pouring energy drinks into her mouth from the corner of the ring. She'd tell him that I had told her he was awful, and he would tell her why I was wrong, and then she'd tell him all the other things I'd told her to say. Afterwards I'd ask her how it went, and she'd go silent on me for a couple of days and then she'd say that they were back together and working things out.

'Henry doesn't think gay people should be allowed to have children,' Amelia said.

'What does he even mean, shouldn't be *allowed* to have children? Who's he imagining should be in charge of gay uteruses?'

'Oh, no, he just means, children need a mother and a father,' Amelia said. And then she said, 'He's being stupid. I've told him he's being stupid.'

You always have this feeling that weddings should be dramatic but in fact, of course, they're extremely dull. Or at least, that was how I felt. I had this expectation – more of a hope, admittedly – that something dramatic would happen at Amelia's wedding, that somebody would interrupt the ceremony to say that Henry was already married or something. When I voiced this to Tati before I left, she'd looked appalled and said, 'But don't you want your friend to be happy?' and I'd said, yes, I did, that was the point. When I voiced it to my grandmother, she'd said, 'Sounds about right.'

I looked around at the people filling the pews: Henry's chinless friends from school and slick colleagues from the law firm, his walking Hogarth sketch of a great uncle who was a hereditary peer and had once spoken passionately in the House of Lords in favour of the right to smoke in a private vehicle in the presence of children. There were Amelia's more ordinary-looking friends, her parents who seemed proud and anxious and honestly a little drunk, her younger cousins fiddling with their flower-girl dresses. I wondered which of them would be the one to do something dramatic, as the service rolled onwards, formally, listlessly, towards the point when I would give the reading.

At first, nobody did anything dramatic, and then, later, nobody did anything dramatic.

I had this daydream, as the vicar announced that we would now stand for the groom's favourite hymn, which was 'Jerusalem', and the congregation began to sing: when it was time for me to do the reading, Amelia would catch my eye and hold it, and while I went through the motions of saying the words, she and I would be having a long, silent conversation that went like this: *I know you think I am making a mistake,* Amelia's eyes would say. *You are making a mistake,* I'd reply. *I know I am making a mistake,* Amelia would say. And at the end of the reading, having communicated all of this through eye contact alone, Amelia would reach out and take my hand (and in this daydream, this was a possibility, my blisters having receded like fog) and we would walk back down the aisle and out of the church together. And everybody would clap.

What's funny is that when it was time for me to do the reading, Amelia *did* catch my eye and hold it, and when I read, 'So I returned, and considered all the oppressions that are done under the sun,' her eyes did say, *I know you think I am making a mistake*. And when I read, 'The fool foldeth his hands together, and eateth his own flesh. Better is an handful with quietness, than both the hands full with travail and vexation of spirit,' her eyes did say, *I know I am making a mistake*.

When I read, 'Two are better than one; because they have a good reward for their labour. For if they fall, the one will lift up his fellow: but woe to him that is alone when he falleth; for he hath not another to help him up,' her eyes said something like, *But where are you? Where are you? Where have you gone?*

'Again, if two lie together, then they have heat: but how can one be warm alone?'

I stopped reading before the line about the old and foolish king, and there was that awkward silence afterwards when you sense that people feel they should clap but know they're not supposed to in church.

I sat down. The couple exchanged their vows.

Amelia did not look at me again.

She and Henry posed for pictures signing the marriage register, holding pens like people who don't know how to hold pens.

We were invited to leave the church and line up outside with confetti.

It was raining when we got outside and the confetti plan was cancelled.

Later, Amelia did not look at me.

Even later than that, Amelia did not look at me.

*

Once, Henry sent me a postcard. He must have got my address from Amelia's phone at some point. It was a picture of the Tower of London. On the back the message read: *Please stop messing with my relationship.*

'Henry thinks it's strange that these people coming over in small boats don't just stay in France,' Amelia said.

'Henry thinks that if the Greeks care so much about the Elgin Marbles, they should have looked after them properly in the first place,' Amelia said.

I came to understand that Amelia told me these things about Henry as a way of making it impossible for her to stay with him, except that she stayed with him and stayed with him and stayed with him.

Once, about a year after she met Henry, Amelia decided to get a kitten. A kitten was the solution to a lot of problems in her life, she said. It was the solution to the problem of not having a kitten, primarily, but also the problem of feeling lonely regardless of whether she and Henry were together or apart. Also, Henry was allergic to cats, so if she got a kitten they would absolutely have to be apart. I was all for it.

We spent a Saturday trawling ads online from people who had cats to sell, and then on Sunday morning took the Overground to Enfield to view a kitten in a tiny flat in one of those very tall tower blocks. The woman who lived there didn't speak much English, but showed us into a bathroom where three kittens were chasing each other in and out of a laundry basket, and we picked them up and pressed our noses into their necks and I couldn't believe how small they were, couldn't stop imagining their tiny bones, their tiny ribs under their fur. Amelia said she'd take the little grey one. She handed over four twenty-pound notes and said we'd be back in a bit, we just had to go and buy a cat carrier.

'And you're sure about this?' I said, as we left the building. 'Are you really, really sure about Henry?'

We took a taxi to a big pet store to buy cat food and a litter tray and things, and then stopped for a coffee. I was bringing the drinks to our table when her phone rang, and even before she answered I knew how it would go. She took the call outside, and I watched her through the window pacing up and down the pavement, her expression shifting from disdain to irritation to tears to, eventually, a small smile, a laugh, a bigger smile. And even though I had known, did know, knew how it would go, I still couldn't quite believe it when she came back and said, 'That was Henry. He wants to talk. If I leave now I can see him before the rugby starts.'

I sat by myself at the table with our coffees in front of me and all the cat stuff by my feet: a huge, heavy bag of litter I had no idea what to do with, a box of felt catnip mice. I thought about the little grey kitten in the bathroom of the flat at the top of the tower block, and I thought about the woman who was waiting for us to go back, and I looked around the cafe in this part of north London where I'd never been before and had no reason to be now, and thought, *What the hell am I doing, what the hell am I doing with my life.*

'What does she see in him, this Henry fellow?' my grandmother asked me, and I said I had no idea. 'Sure you do,' my grandmother said, and I said okay, maybe it was that Henry believed he was better than everyone else, which made Amelia feel better too. Maybe it was because he was so certain of himself. My grandmother said, 'Some people would rather be treated like dirt than be alone,' and maybe that was all there was to it, maybe that was the whole thing.

But how can one be warm alone?

A week or so after the kitten incident, my father called to tell me my grandmother was dying, alone, in Texas, and refusing hospice care. I surprised myself and everyone else when I said I'd be the one to go. She'd moved to Austin in the eighties and I'd only met her a few times, but it felt like a relief to have an obligation to attend to. I quit my job selling heat pumps for an energy company. I gave my landlord notice on the flat. It was startling how simple it was to unlatch myself from my life. I told Amelia I was leaving, casually, as though it had nothing to do with her, and she told me in turn, casually, that Henry had proposed and she'd said yes, as though it had nothing to do with me, which it didn't, of course, and yet.

'Congratulations,' I said.

'I'll miss you,' she said.

After the ceremony, all the guests had to walk down the lane from the church to Henry's family home, where the reception was being held. The wedding party was driven there in a convoy of classic cars, which kept them drier than the rest of us. The rain was really coming down by that point. We scurried along, heads lowered, and ducked into the enormous marquee on the lawn, where there was champagne and a string quartet and nowhere to hide.

I got caught in a stilted conversation with an old man who was wearing a waistcoat and waving a cigar around. I ran out of ways to say hadn't the service been lovely, so asked whether he was a friend of the bride or groom, and he looked at me strangely and said, 'We shall fight on the beaches, we shall fight on the landing grounds, we shall fight in the fields and in the streets, we shall fight in the hills; we shall never surrender.' He said all this very slowly, as though he was speaking to an idiot. When I said nothing, he dug into a pocket and produced a soft-edged business card that read 'Brian Walker, Churchill Impersonator'.

It hadn't crossed my mind that my friend was the type of person who would have a Churchill impersonator at her wedding, but of course she was, because Henry was. I remembered then I'd been told there was some historic link between Churchill and Henry's family home, a famous treaty had been signed in the library there. Presumably the impersonator had been hired to ensure this was not forgotten.

I excused myself and left the marquee, pretending to look for the loos. There was a big arch with stone lions flanking it and roses bobbing under the weight of the rain. On the other side was another courtyard, the ivied facade of the main house at one end. Posing in front of it was Amelia, and Henry, and the bridesmaids.

The bridesmaids' blue dresses flapped around their legs and turned dark grey in the rain. Their hair, curled and crowned, was blowing across their faces. They must have decided to embrace the bad weather for the photos, because they were waving white umbrellas around and laughing, and Henry was holding his jacket over my friend's head, ineffectively but in a way that looked gallant. They were facing me but looking at the photographer, and they didn't seem to notice I was there. I considered reversing slowly before they did, but it was too late and Amelia called out my name, and I had to smile and gesture helplessly in a way that I hoped conveyed that I was simply looking for the loos.

I saw myself as they must have seen me, looming oddly out of the rain at a moment that was not supposed to include me.

I thought about swimming with Amelia, those slow lengths in the pool, passing each other halfway, and the brush of her toes against mine and how I had never really known what to say to her, what magic combination of words would release us from what we were locked into.

The rain felt good on my hands. They weren't itching any more.

And as I trod my way back towards the car park in the village, I thought about my life in Texas, about my grandmother dying slowly and pragmatically among the chickens and the wind chimes, about Tati and the way her hair got in my face when we slept and how much I liked that, actually, and about how much larger the world felt there: the enormous weather, the enormous sky, the enormous whole-body jolt of possibility I occasionally felt, the possibility that, being somewhere else, I could become someone else, or more strikingly still, a person more like myself than I had been before, at home, with Amelia.

A day was coming when I would go in to wake my grandmother and find she was unwakeable. And another, a little while later, when Tati would say we needed to talk and then say she really liked me as a person but she didn't really see this going anywhere and we should probably just be friends. And I'd find myself alone in a big place and I'd have to decide what to do next.

I walked on through the rain.

The yoga studio I'd been to before leaving for the wedding was near my grandmother's bungalow. It was one of a small cluster of businesses beside an enormous parking lot; I had to cross two main roads to get there. Tati had recommended it and even though I'd never done yoga before, and even though I felt sceptical about the whole thing, I was keen to impress her, so I went. It was the only place I'd been in Austin without air conditioning: they kept the doors open, front and back, so there was a constant thrum of traffic that sounded, when I closed my eyes, like the ocean.

I paid two dollars to rent a mat and a cork block and some

sort of rope. You had to spray down the mat before and after using it, the woman at the front desk said, and she showed me where the bottle and cloths were. And then the instructor sort of floated through the door, all limbs and American-white smile and incredibly clean hair, ushering us into the room where the class would take place, and we began, stretching tall and flopping over to touch our toes and twisting one elbow onto the opposite knee, all the while breathing to a slow and steady count of five: in, in, out, out, out. When I breathed in I could smell the rubbery mat and the cleaning spray and all the dead skin that had been pressed into its crevices by the people who'd rented it before, and it wasn't disgusting or unpleasant or anything like that; it felt close and ordinary and like being part of something. The room was mirrored on all four sides and there was no escaping yourself, whichever way you looked: there I was, and there I was, and there I was.

I thought about the journey to the wedding the next day, rehearsing in my mind the flight, the drive, the service and the reading. And – in, in – I tried to tell myself that all I had to do was get the reading right – out, out, out – and that after that, Amelia and I could fade from each other's lives – in, in – and that I would be happy and so would she – I breathed out, out, out – and that we could still want that for each other from afar. I ran through Ecclesiastes 4 in my head, which I realised then I knew by heart. The words fell in time to my breathing. And when the instructor told us to move into downward-facing dog she put her hand on the small of my back to guide me into the correct position and said, 'Now ground yourself, really push your palms into the mat,' and I did. 'That's it,' she said, 'that's it, that's right, that's wonderful,' and when my skin began to tingle, I thought what I was feeling was triumph.

Strike

Iris was not much of a striker, which is what she said when really pushed to comment. She had paid her fees to the University and College Union, not enthusiastically, but because who knew, these days, whether your job was safe, whether you might, at the next department board meeting, discover that student recruitment had fallen for the sixth year in a row (government policy pushing girls into STEM; boys never had much interest anyway) and there would be redundancies before the year was out? Still, she had not voted for the strike – had not voted at all. The ballot paper had arrived; she had put it on top of a pile of letters to deal with at some point, and then, when she had looked for it a week or so later, it wasn't there. It must have gone into the recycling.

Of the union members who had voted, though, the majority were in favour, and the strike was called. Iris had received multiple emails about it, first from the union, saying that staff were under no obligation to announce in advance whether or not they would deliver teaching during the strike period, then from HR, demanding that staff announce in advance whether or not they would deliver teaching during the strike period. She had filed everything in her 'strike' folder, which contained similar emails from the dispute two years ago. She had not been much of a striker then, either.

Her preference, in this situation and all others, was to carry on as normal. She liked term time. Liked teaching. Honestly, she even liked marking, which was a fact she had learned to keep to herself, as her colleagues tended to react with horror. During the strike, however, there was no normal to be carried on with. She was within her rights to continue teaching regardless, but could not bring herself to cross the picket line. There would be people she knew there, who would have spoken to her personally or held it against her; God forbid, there might be people she *admired* there. So her approach had always been to spend strike days catching up on emails at home, or in the British Library doing research: not not striking, but not striking either.

She hated the sight of the picket lines, that was for sure. There was something about their aesthetics. The art history department always came up with particularly aggravating visual jokes on their placards: *'Ceci n'est pas une PICKET'*; *The Birth of Venus*, except Venus was wearing a red UCU armband; an eye-rolling medieval baby Jesus under the words 'When you have a zero-hours contract and your employer expects you to work weekends for free.' Worst of all: the Van Gogh puns. These were the bottom of the barrel, the least inspired, and especially irritating because there was no consensus on the pronunciation of 'Gogh', so that the same picket line could include both 'Keep (Van) Gogh-ing, Comrades!' and 'Keep your hands (Van) Gogh our pensions!' Intolerable.

All of which meant that on the first day of the strike, Iris was furious – kicking herself, really – to discover that she had left her medication in the office fridge. She had planned a working-from-home day: comfortable clothes and plenty of quality time with Dr Gachet, her gingery, long-faced border terrier adopted from Battersea. She had bought a mini quiche from the bakery for lunch; had cancelled the dog walker. But now there was this medication emergency. There was no getting around it. She had left the drugs in the shared fridge on the third floor, in a brown paper bag on which she had scrawled her name and a warning: PRIVATE. She had checked her own fridge at home in case there was a spare box at the back, lurking behind jars of mustard and mayonnaise, but found nothing. The last of her supply was in the work fridge, and she was due her next injection at 11 a.m., which was in just under two hours' time. The timings of the doses, her doctor had emphasised, had to be exact. There was nothing for it but to go into work, to cross the picket.

Iris told herself: she was not much of a striker, anyway.

Part of what irked Iris about the Van Gogh picket signs was that it positioned him in among the fray, when, as far as she was concerned, he had always been alone, on the outside of things, looking in. Her colleagues had no right putting him in with all the others, as though he was like everyone else. (Iris went so far, sometimes, as to think of herself as Vincent's only friend.) She had devoted her life to him, certainly. Had spent a year learning Dutch during her PhD just to read his letters. Had written a monograph about him: *Pine Trees by the Walls of the Asylum: Peripheralities and framing in the Van*

Gogh correspondence. One hundred thousand words, not just about him, or even about his art, but about his writing, and this very specific thing *about* his writing: peripheralities (not technically a word, but the kind of thing that could be got away with), the stuff at the edges, the marginalia of a man who in his own lifetime had been entirely marginal, and was now mainstream, no longer edgy. As the picket signs attested, he had become a meme.

Which was not to say that she had no sense of outrage or solidarity with the picketers. She had a great sense of both, in fact; she was outraged by all sorts of things. It was just the awkwardness of it, having to look your students in the eye – students who were paying thousands of pounds they didn't have just to be there – and say that your principles dictated that you should not provide the service they had paid for. Never mind that their attendance was patchy at the best of times. Never mind that they seemed, year on year, to grow ever less motivated, ever less interested in actually learning. Never mind their moods or motivations at all. They had paid for an education, and whether or not they made use of it was up to them.

Think of it this way, she reasoned to herself as she arrived at the bus stop: if you were to buy a car, even if you had no intention whatsoever of driving it, you should be able to rely on the fact that the car would always be yours. It started to rain, cold enough that it was almost sleet. The bus arrived.

Iris's commute took ninety minutes on a good day: a bus to the Tube, a Tube to the overground, and then a train all the way across the city to the suburb where the university was. She preferred to live far away from work; it gave her a healthy sense of separation, and she never ran into students or colleagues. She liked the brief immersion into the rest of the world on her way between her home and her office.

She felt particularly glad, that day, that her journey to work was so long. She was in no rush to arrive and confront the fracas of the strike. But as she disembarked the bus and entered the Tube, descending on the escalator into the murky underground air, it struck her that on this occasion she was making alarmingly good time. She checked her watch. She had banked on having at least the usual ninety minutes to come up with a plan for how to cross the picket line under the radar. (What plan, exactly, she couldn't imagine, there being only one route in and out of the art history department, and no option other than keeping her head down, politely excusing herself to get past the signs and the people waving them, picking up the medication, injecting herself in the ladies' loos and then getting the hell out of there.)

A moment of madness: she could just get off the Tube, give up on the plan and on the medication altogether. Eleven a.m. could come and go with no injection, which would inevitably mean that the whole cycle would be ruined. Perhaps it would be worth it. She pondered the possibility, imagined ascending the escalator, the rain-slicked concourse with its CAUTION – SLIPPERY signs, the walk back home, conflict avoided, the long day and long evening with nothing to do, no little vials to remove from the fridge, no syringes to draw the liquid from one and mix it with the powder in another. There would be no need for the ritual of grabbing the fleshiest part of her stomach and sliding the needle into it. She always felt as though she was going to burst when she did this: her body just a balloon in the shape of a woman. There would be no need for the sharps box, with its tittering rattle. She felt giddy at the thought of giving up on all of it, of throwing her hands up in the air and saying, *To hell with pickets, syringes and the baby thing.*

The baby thing. She thought about Van Gogh, as of course she always did, and about a line he had written in a letter to his brother: *Oh God, where is my wife, oh God, where is my child, is being alone really living?* It popped into her head all the time, this line, as she was marking essays, for example, or washing up. Waiting for her computer to turn on: *Oh God, where is my wife?* Tidying up the unused handouts and used coffee cups left behind by students after a lecture: *Oh God, where is my child?* Sorting through her clean laundry trying to pair up socks. Doing the stomach injections, pushing in the plunger, as the liquid began to sting her from the inside. *Is being alone really living?* Brushing her teeth.

No, there was nothing for it but to get the drugs. Without the drugs, there was no possibility of a baby. And without the possibility of a baby, would she be really living?

The previous year, she had viewed a nice two-bed flat: it was within budget and the location was only slightly inconvenient. The estate agent drove her there in his glistening black car, footwell strewn with sweet wrappers. When he had parked and she was twisting in her seat to get out, he said, 'Just one thing.' For a terrifying moment, she thought he was hitting on her. 'I'd just ask you to be sensitive about the second bedroom,' he said. 'The current owners are home, so we'll just look in on that room quickly. I'd ask you not to comment on it.'

Perhaps the room had a terrible smell, she had thought. Perhaps a moody teenaged son was holed up in there, masturbating into socks and farting without restraint. Or someone with a rare and upsetting medical condition. A dying grandmother. A madwoman in the second bedroom.

'Of course,' she said, giving a small nod.

She was on edge looking around the flat, which turned out to be delightful: tastefully decorated and spacious, even a little patch of grass out the back where Dr Gachet could do his business. The owners were sat on the sofa watching television: a couple in their mid-thirties, she guessed, younger than she was in any case. They didn't look away from the screen when Iris and the estate agent came in, or acknowledge in any way that there were people in their home.

'There's a decent-sized bathroom,' the estate agent said, gesturing that she should follow him down a corridor. 'And,' he affected a casual tone, 'here's the second bedroom.' He opened the door a crack. Iris's heart hammered.

The room was small, and full of baby things. There was a crib, a buggy, a bouncer, mounds of tiny clothes, all higgledy-piggledy, thrown into heaps. The cot was piled high with stuffed toys, a car seat tilting at an angle. The doorway was partially blocked by a cardboard box full of unopened packs of nappies.

She took it all in quickly, then stepped back and hurried to admire the bathroom. She felt a little sick: all that baby stuff and no baby, like Vincent's paintings of empty chairs, boots without feet, portraits of anticipation, a way of saying: *Someone will be here soon, won't they?* A way of saying: *Is being alone really living?* (A darting thought: her own reproductive system as equally horrifying, baby stuff without a baby in it.) She could hear the television playing in the living room, but she sensed that the owners' attention was focused entirely on her.

'Oh,' she said, 'I love the tiles. The blue glaze.' And then she made a quick exit from the flat. The estate agent, who looked about twelve years old, said nothing more about it as he drove them to the next place, but everywhere else they saw that day was either too small or too expensive, and the whole time she was distracted, thinking about the baby room, about the silent owners and the daytime TV and the way they had been so quiet and so alert and had given nothing away.

She would later be ashamed of her first assumption, which was that the woman who lived there was crazy, that she had an imaginary baby and kept buying things for it. Iris assumed that the man, embarrassed, hid it all in the second bedroom when there were viewings. When she thought it through: of course, the couple's baby had died. The baby was dead and they had not been able to bring themselves to throw anything away. The baby was dead.

She tried not to wonder what it said about her that she had concocted the other scenario first, the one in which the woman was insane.

She had not taken the flat.

*

Iris's own dead babies ran the whole gamut from barely there blastocysts to solid-limbed, embodied, alien-looking creatures with faces. There were not so many that she could not remember each discretely: one emerged at thirteen weeks; there was an outlier at eighteen weeks with fingers clenched in gluey fists. Once, when a twelve-week scan had revealed a foetus with no heartbeat, she'd had surgery to remove what doctors referred to as 'the products of conception', and the hospital had offered to arrange a funeral. She had thought, at first, that this was a tasteless joke, but it really was something people did. It would be at the local crematorium, the nurse explained; the hospital had an arrangement with them for the first Tuesday of every month. Iris said she did not require a funeral for the products of conception. In general, she flushed her miscarriages down the toilet.

The final leg of her journey, the overground, was steamy. The weather had worsened and spatters of sleet were hitting the windows. The panes had fogged up. Teenagers had doodled hearts and initials. A pigeon had shuffled into the carriage and was pecking around at lurid orange crumbs spilling from a crisp packet. A man in a suit jerked his foot at it. A woman took a photo on her phone.

Oh, give me the freedom to be a bird like other birds, Vincent once wrote, flappably, crawling out of his own odd skin.

Iris checked her watch: it was ten fifteen. She had forty-five minutes to get the medication and inject it, which was plenty of time, she thought, more than enough. Too much, if anything.

The pigeon disembarked at the next stop and was replaced by a woman with a double buggy: a toddler and baby side by side, both gazing blankly ahead through the rain-beaded plastic cover. Iris stared then looked away.

The baby thing, more than anything, was just so embarrassing. Nobody expected it of her. Her sister and parents, beloved and slightly, really ever so slightly different from her, did not expect it. They had watched with nothing but pride as she had grown from a serious child into a serious adult. Her sisters, who were sporty and arty respectively, had neither understood nor judged her, had invited her to parties with them and been unsurprised when she declined. Her parents had never asked the kinds of awkward questions about boyfriends that other people's parents seemed to.

It wasn't until she started her PhD that the differences between her and her family became stark. In the four years it took to complete her thesis, her sisters between them produced five offspring. The youngest got married. The oldest divorced. Her siblings' lives seemed, from the outside, at once stolid and unstable. Her own, by comparison, remained flimsy but became focused. Conference papers. Seminars in anonymous, grey rooms. The brittle quiet of the library. Endless applications for fellowships and scholarships and research funding. Zero-hours teaching contracts. Leading listless undergraduates through the sculpture hall at the V&A. And then this, her job, which had been offered to her just when she was thinking of giving up and moving home, becoming a project manager like her older sister, or a marketing co-ordinator, like her younger.

When she had signed the contract with the university and was formally employed, she felt tired. No thrill, no triumph, no celebration. Just an overwhelming urge to curl up inside this sudden, yearned-for security and fall asleep in it.

Security. How funny that she had thought that's what it was, as though a job could protect against all the other horrors of life. As though even a job could protect her from the possibility of not having a job. There wasn't a year since she'd started when redundancies weren't being muttered about, when retirees were not replaced and everybody had to take on extra lectures, when there hadn't been angry emails from the union about this problem or that problem: pensions, precarity, workload.

When there hadn't been strikes, there had been the threat of strikes. It all exhausted her in equal measure: the determined decline of higher education, and the efforts to prevent it. Maybe it would have been easier to get worked up about, if it weren't for the baby thing.

She was forty-three years old. She had spent, oh, almost everything she'd ever earned on the baby thing. And now she was old enough that nobody expected it of her, and in fact most people treated it with a sort of hushed respect, her babyless-ness. Sometimes they apologised for their own children as though she might be offended by noise and dirt and chaos and tiny hands. As though she were above it. As though she had chosen a higher purpose, on purpose.

Oh God, where is my wife, oh God, where is my child, is being alone really living?

*

The sleet was rain again by the time the overground arrived at the stop nearest the university. Iris shuffled up the steps towards the exit, already feeling self-conscious, as though it was perfectly obvious from her face or her clothes or her manner what she was there to do. She checked the time: half past ten. The walk to the department took about ten minutes, and she found herself dragging her feet.

At first there had been Robert, and he had been in on the baby thing, too. They had met at a conference, and had gone out for a year and a half before getting married slightly awkwardly. They both felt marriage, like almost everything else in life, was embarrassing. But it had seemed like a nice thing to do and they had done it, and shortly after that had agreed that the next embarrassing thing they wanted was a baby. Iris tried not to think about it too much. And then, after just over a year with no success, she found that she definitely had thought about it too much, had unknowingly become fluent in a new language: ovulation windows, the varying qualities of cervical mucus, hideous euphemistic acronyms used on internet forums, like 'BD', which stood for 'baby dancing', which was what a certain kind of person online preferred to say in place of 'having sex'. *We BD'd every day during my OW and still got a BFN today.*

Once, Robert had decided to run a half marathon, and for a while all he could think or talk about was negative splits and pronation stabilisation, and Iris remembered thinking it was as though he had been translated into the most boring version of himself. She felt that way about herself now, with the baby thing: it was her turn to be translated.

BFN. Big fat negative. It was horrible, humiliating, really, and yet it became the defining term of that period of her life. Negative after negative, big and fat and repeated monthly. Occasionally, the test showed two lines instead of one – positive – and she would be pregnant for a little while, and then not pregnant any more.

Vincent wrote: *How much sadness there is in life.*

She and Robert were both examined: scanned and prodded, blood drawn. It turned out Robert had slightly sluggish sperm, so for a while they thought it was that. She had a heart-shaped uterus, which was also considered a bad thing. The ideal uterus, she learned, was shaped like a sweet potato. There was the waiting list for fibroid surgery, and then there was fibroid surgery, and then recovery from it. There was the waiting list for IVF, and then there was IVF. The NHS gave them two cycles. Two! Which had seemed like plenty, bountiful even. She had imagined the babies being bestowed upon them, two per round at least, or more! Twins! Triplets! An all-you-can-eat baby buffet. The initial process of receiving and refrigerating the medications, learning how to inject them into her stomach, attending scans every other morning, sedation for egg collection, full bladder for embryo transfer: she had been delighted by all of it, really game for it. She had felt lucky.

Vincent wrote: *I am turning into a dog.*

Over time, that was how she felt, too. Hang dog.

They blew through their two free rounds of IVF with no luck, and went private. The prices at the fertility clinic on Harley Street gave her a kind of vertigo: almost a third of her annual salary, just for one round. They pooled their savings and took the plunge, saying things like, 'Third time's the charm,' and, 'You've got to be in it to win it,' and other phrases they would never normally use. If they had started the adoption process when her parents had first mentioned it, she thought, they might have a baby already. But they had not started it. They did not have a baby.

Dog tired. She started avoiding her nephews and nieces. Her sisters sent their best wishes for her research, which was, she told them, taking up all of her time.

The first private cycle yielded three embryos. They transferred the first, and she miscarried. Dogged, they transferred the second. It didn't work. The third made it to twelve weeks before she started cramping and bleeding.

They took out a loan. They paid for two more cycles. Dog with a bone.

By this point, she found that she would look at Robert and feel absolutely nothing at all. She could not remember the feeling of wanting him, or even of wanting a baby *with him*. Sometimes she couldn't tell if she even wanted a baby. IVF was just a thing they were doing. It felt compulsory, like homework. They did not bother having sex any more.

'I am turning into a dog,' she said to Robert. He rolled over in bed so his back was to her. 'Robert,' she said. 'Robert.'

They stopped talking. Let sleeping dogs lie.

After the divorce, she carried on with donor sperm, buying cycles whenever she could afford it, because she did not remember how not to try.

She thought of IVF, in her more rational moments, as an expensive gambling habit.

Vincent wrote: *It won't do for us to think that I am completely sane.*

Sometimes she fantasised about *finding* a baby – stumbling across one, in fact – on a doorstep or a park bench, a lost baby, perhaps with a note: *Please take care of this baby.* In a different mood, she imagined finding a corpse while out walking Dr Gachet. No reason, really. Just for the thrill of it.

There was a flow of people moving towards the university. Iris only noticed once she had been part of it for a few moments. Students with signs. A few older people, academics presumably. Somebody thrust a flyer at her: there was a rally in support of the strike, it said, starting in the courtyard outside the central building at eleven o'clock.

It was quarter to eleven when Iris arrived on campus. Crowds were gathering in front of the main entrance: a collage of umbrellas. To the right was the building that housed the art history department, and in front of it, sheltering under the eaves, was the picket line. There was a sign that read 'Official UCU Picket'. People were standing around it in groups, some smoking, some on their phones, others jumping forward to hand out stickers to passers-by. She spotted several of her PhD students in a cluster, heads bent towards each other. The medievalists were standing together; one of them was telling a joke and the rest were waiting for the moment when they should laugh. Even the head of department was there, for God's sake, deep in conversation with Josephine Lee, who lectured in nineteenth-century French visual cultures and had her kids with her: a rotund 3-year-old at her knees and a baby on her hip. Both children were wearing UCU shirts.

Iris's stomach knotted as she took in the mass of bodies blocking the route from where she stood on the road to the fridge on the third floor. She felt exposed, pelted by rain and in plain view, as though she were without cover during a shoot-out. She began to retreat around the corner to collect herself, looking back at the picket to check there really was no easy way around it. And of course, of course, just at that moment Josephine Lee happened to glance in her direction. Their eyes met. Josephine's face lit up with a smile and there was nowhere for Iris to hide; Josephine had a clean shot.

'Iris! Iris! Over here!' Josephine shunted her baby up on her hip and waved.

Iris pretended she hadn't seen anything, pretended she couldn't hear her name being called. She checked her watch for some reason, as though she was late for something (and, God, how was it six minutes to eleven all of a sudden?) She looked up at the sky. The rain was black from below.

'Iris!' Josephine called, and then her toddler joined in with a crackling, cartoony, 'I-wiss! I-wiss!'

Iris thought she might burst into tears. It had been hopeless all along, this mission. She was always going to get caught, always going to have to explain to her earnest colleagues that she was not much of a striker, because she'd rather say that than explain anything else, and watch their faces as they recalibrated their opinion of her. She was always going to find herself damp and red-faced in the draughty ladies' loos, injecting her stomach while the sound of shouted slogans drifted up through a window that was permanently jammed open, dreading having to walk past them again on her way out. The journey home was always going to be a meditation on humiliation.

She ran a hand across her stomach, seeking out bruises from the previous day's needles. She found one and pressed down on it.

She turned to face the picket. Smiled. Waved.

'Hi,' she called. 'I'm not actually – well, you see, I'm not much of a—'

There was an incident – Iris thought of it as the Lamp Incident –when Vincent had been a young man, which came to mind then, as she locked eyes with Josephine Lee and forced herself to walk forwards.

Vincent had asked his cousin, Kee, to marry him, to which she had responded (Iris found it easy to imagine her as she said it, lifting her eyes to meet his with a taut, frustrated sigh) 'Never, no, never.' For someone other than Vincent, perhaps that would have been the end of it.

Instead: Vincent burst into the house of his aunt and uncle during dinner one evening, and stuck his hand in the flame of a lamp. The family watched aghast as Vincent announced he would not move: he wanted to see Kee and would burn until he did. There must have been a smell, Iris supposed; the hairs on the back of his hand singeing. There must have been a spreading red stain on Vincent's knuckles.

A moment of surprised silence. Then, Vincent's aunt bent

forwards and blew out the flame. There would have been a shock of cold air where the heat had been, and a tightening of the skin; the beginnings of a blister forming. How strange, Iris thought, how dizzying it must have been, to decide to be on fire, and find that you are not.

Iris thought so often about this – the lamp, the hand interrupting the flame, how quickly and mortifyingly it was all over – that she sometimes felt as though it had happened to her. It was her hand, she caught herself thinking. Her hair that was burning. It was her shock at the hot-skin sting, and her rage when that pain was suddenly gone, replaced by nothing at all.

From under the eaves of the department building, the rain sounded like applause. It felt warmer there, too, though Iris was shivery. She made a concerted effort to lower her shoulders from near her ears. The picketers, up close, reminded her of pigeons that nestled under the bridge near her flat, cooing to each other and watching foot traffic. There was a sort of grim cosiness to it.

'Iris,' Josephine said, as soon as she was close enough. 'How lovely that you're here.'

'No,' said Iris, gesturing towards the door. 'No – I'm not—'

But by then the head of department had muscled in, saying, 'You need an armband from Bill. Bill! Get Iris an armband!'

Oh God, Iris thought, *where is my wife, oh God, where is my child, is being—*

But Bill, a Seurat specialist whom Iris had never particularly liked, was handing her a red armband, and the head of department was saying, 'Great stuff,' and the medievalists had paused their conversation to wave at her, and Josephine was saying, 'Would you like to hold my sign?' The sign was leaning against the wall: just a low-quality printout of Munch's *The Scream* stuck to some cardboard and that was it, not even any words.

'No,' said Iris. She checked her watch. Eleven. 'No, I'm not – I'm not—'

'Oh, actually,' Josephine said, 'could you hold Charlie, then, just for a second? I need to take Bella to the loo. Is that all right?'

And Josephine was extending the baby towards her, expectantly, the child's legs dangling like a pair of exclamation marks. He was missing a sock: pink toes almost spherical, foot creased with fat. His little UCU top had a stain down the front.

'Is that all right?' Josephine repeated, and Iris had said nothing, had not said it was all right, had been about to say that she was not much of a striker, actually, but then Josephine was leading her toddler towards the department door, and Iris found that she was left holding the baby, his head on her shoulder, his back surprisingly firm. She patted him. She bobbed up and down like a buoy, or a person drowning. The baby's hands flailed, his fingers cold and sticky whenever they brushed her face.

'Hush,' she said, though he wasn't crying, and then to nobody, or to the baby, she said, 'I don't – I'm not—' and stopped.

The university clock tower, which ran three minutes

late, chimed eleven, and the crowd that had gathered in the courtyard began to shuffle and murmur, and the head of department said to Iris, expectantly, 'We're all going over, now, to join the rally,' and Iris looked back through the building's glass door to the illuminated buttons by the lifts. She imagined getting in one, sliding up to the third floor, and she thought about the fridge there, about her medication in its brown paper bag, next to someone's out-of-date yogurt and a horizontal bottle of wine left over from a seminar.

In the courtyard, a man with a megaphone had started a chant, a call and response that the crowd was calling-and-responding to, rambunctious, excited, and the rain was easing off a little and there was no sign of Josephine, who would be a few more minutes at least, and what was there for Iris to do except stay there among the crowd and become one of the strikers after all, refusing to carry on (with work, with plans, with all the ideas she'd had about what she was going to accomplish and become)? What was there to do except move off with everyone else towards the rally and the noise? The baby seemed oblivious to all of it, had fallen asleep, his face completely still against her collarbone, his lips sheened with dribble, and it was past eleven now in any case.

Was being alone really living?

Iris couldn't make out what the crowd was chanting, so she shouted whatever sprang to mind, which was, 'It is!' The words tasted strange in her mouth, and uncertain, but since it was so loud, there were so many people all around her and none of them minded at all what she was saying, she tried again, and louder: 'It is! It is!'

Pulse

'Hmm?' you said. 'What did you say?'

All evening, I'd been trying and failing to raise it. I'd been gulping air whenever conversation lulled, ready but not ready to blurt it out. I'd been starting the sentence and then losing my nerve, diverting to something innocuous. It had been on the tip of my tongue the whole time, but I'd been biting it. And when I finally built up the courage to tell you, you didn't hear what I'd said.

We'd finished dinner. You were washing up.

I repeated myself. 'I want to go to Warsaw.'

You flipped a dirty plate over in the water and slid the sponge across it.

Bubbles slid off the white ridges on the bottom of the dish.

I clarified. 'I'm going, in fact. To Warsaw. This weekend. I already booked the flight.'

You slotted the plate into the drying rack and wiped your hands on a tea towel. Then, finally, you turned around.

'Why?' you said. I was convinced you'd look annoyed. Instead, you only looked bemused.

It was absolutely the right question to ask.

We both knew there were a lot of reasons why I shouldn't

go to Warsaw. Among them: we had already made plans to see friends that weekend; we were supposed to be saving money; I was a nervous traveller who, even on our honeymoon, got homesick and wanted to leave early; I had no sense of direction and was always getting lost; I had no connection to Warsaw and had never previously mentioned a desire to go; we had a lot to do around the house to get it ready for the baby; you were, at that point, twenty-one weeks pregnant and feeling tired all the time.

I joined you at the sink, sliding my wine glass into the washing-up bowl. 'I want to do it before the baby comes. Just a quick trip. Just a weekend.'

'Why?' you said again.

Air bubbled up from the glass, then it sank below the froth of Fairy liquid.

What I said was, 'I want to listen to Chopin's heart.'

I had been learning the piano, at that point, for ten years. I started casually, quite soon after we got fake-married. I had just turned twenty-four and you were still a graduate student, writing your PhD on American road-trip narratives. We lived in a top-floor flat that got too hot in summer and I had a job as an assistant manager at a cafe inside a petrol station just outside of town. Every day I would drive to work, leaving you at your desk at the window, and I'd come back to find you still there, head down. The post would be unopened on the doormat, the carpet flecked with moulted fur from the elderly Siamese cat we inherited from your grandmother. I would kiss the top of your head and retreat into the bedroom to practise.

I taught myself using online tutorials and an electric keyboard balanced on the ironing board. It was the kind that came with sound effects: cymbals, a drum beat. There was a button you could press to play the entirety of the *Moonlight Sonata*. I wore headphones so I didn't disturb you, and practised scales, shaky and unsure: C major, G major, D major. Arpeggios. I tried stretching my fingers out to span an octave, then further. I wished my hands were bigger. It didn't feel important, but it didn't feel unimportant either.

When you asked me why I wanted to play the piano I was furious, full of spluttered indignation. *Look what you have,* I wanted to say. *You have all those American road trips to think about: Kerouac and Steinbeck and Route 66 and Thelma and Louise. Sometimes when I get home you don't even look up from what you're writing! And what do I have? Car-wash tokens and watery instant cappuccinos and bouquets of carnations wilting outside the kiosk and everything smelling of petrol, even things that are nothing to do with petrol, even me.* What I actually said was something about a creative outlet.

For my twenty-fifth birthday, you gave me an electric piano with weighted keys, designed to respond to touch like real ivory. It had a sustain pedal that plugged in at the back. You asked to hear me play. I said I wasn't ready.

For my twenty-sixth birthday, you gave me a piano stool, velvety as a ring box. You opened the lid and it was like you were proposing all over again. Inside was a stash of old sheet music you said was there when you bought it. Crisp, dusty pages of Mozart. Bach. Debussy. Chopin's *Nocturnes*. I stared at the notes: semiquavers crushed between the neat lines of the staves, like ants emerging from a crack in the pavement. I could play none of it: my fingers too slow, my brain too sluggish.

When you finished your doctorate, you were offered a job at a university on the other side of the country. We packed up the house: pot plants; all the clothes we'd forgotten we owned and which probably didn't fit us any more; the books you had written about in your thesis; the little round cat bed, unused since the Siamese cat had died, but which we should keep, you said, because we might get kittens. On moving day, I carried the keyboard out to the van and you put your hand on my arm and said, 'No need to bring that.' I was ready to argue, but you carried on: 'There's a surprise waiting for you in the new house.' I left the keyboard on the pavement with a note that said 'Free to a good home'. The surprise in the new house was a rickety old upright with red candle-wax stains down the side. The A flat below middle C was permanently stuck down. It was beautiful. I almost cried. I loved it for its haphazardness, for its weight and clout and not-plugged-in-ness. Its keys were yellowed, like a smoker's smile.

I was twenty-nine by then, had been playing for five years and had mastered the basics. I could handle some Mozart sonatas and a few simple Bach pieces. I could be relied upon to accompany the singing of 'Happy Birthday' at parties. You had a salary from the university, and I got a job as the manager of a cafe at a National Trust property: it meant I could afford a piano teacher, who came to the house for an hour every Tuesday morning and told me my technique was all wrong, that we would have to start from scratch, all the way back to the C major scale.

Then same-sex marriage was legalised and we got real-married. I played an arrangement of 'I'd Rather Go Blind' by Etta James on the grand piano in the town hall. At the reception, you had too much champagne. You got giggly. You whispered, 'I want a baby. Let's have a baby.'

After two years of lessons, my piano teacher let me open the crinkled copy of Chopin's *Nocturnes* and play the easiest one: No. 2 in E flat major, Op. 9.

When I finally mastered it, I couldn't stop playing it; there was so much inside the music, so much just under the surface. I noticed you humming it to yourself as you moved around the house, getting dressed, straightening a picture frame on the wall, reaching up to open the curtains. By then, you were three months pregnant with our child, just beginning to show: light streaming in behind you and your silhouette, ridiculous, too beautiful, too much to bear.

At the airport I stood, foolishly, beneath the signs that said 'Departures' and 'Arrivals'. I was departing for Warsaw from the airport at which I had just arrived. I had no sense at all of which I should report to. This was the sort of thing you knew. Whenever we'd travelled before, I had followed you unthinkingly, without noticing there had ever been a choice about where to walk.

The phrase 'new arrival' lodged itself in my head. It was the name of the magazine they kept in the waiting room at the fertility clinic: *New Arrivals*. Each edition had a different pink-cheeked, beaming baby on the cover. There were headlines like 'Twelve fertility myths debunked!' and 'Is freezing embryos the future of IVF?' You would flick through them and point at things you thought were helpful or stupid, and then a nurse would call us in.

New arrival. The phrase made me think of the baby as coming *from* somewhere. As though the baby was, at present, sitting in the departure lounge of a faraway airport, rather than doing what it definitely was doing: unfurling, twitchily, right there inside you.

This train of thought made me certain – almost certain – that I should follow the 'Departures' sign. I set off in that direction, then doubted myself and asked a woman in a fluorescent jacket. She looked me up and down. I felt self-conscious, suddenly, about my shoes, which were old, the sole on the left one coming loose. Her expression said: *You should know that; who doesn't know that? You should just give up on whatever this scheme is and go home.* Then she waved me on in the direction I'd been heading.

This scheme was, at most, a blip. A research trip (though you might ask, reasonably enough, what the purpose of the research was; what book did I think I was writing; what conference would hear my academic paper). I tried to think of it, at the time, as a weekend away: the thing that people who aren't me might call *me time*. It was reasonable, wasn't it, as motherhood approached with all its attendant responsibilities, to want to take a minibreak, to visit the home of a composer whose music I loved? Other people did similar things: Stratford-upon-Avon; Oscar Wilde's tomb in Père Lachaise cemetery, peppered with lipstick kisses. Not so strange, then, to want to visit the city of Chopin's birth. A little stranger, I will admit: the heart thing.

Now, years later, you sometimes refer to it as 'that time you left when I was pregnant'. You say it gruffly, a little morosely: 'It was a while after that time you left.' Or, 'It was around the time you went away.' And it's true there was a moment when I left, or several moments really, one of which involved me standing confused beneath the airport signs, an inexperienced traveller who had never before gone anywhere by myself, shuffling through security towards the gate. But as soon as the plane took off for Warsaw, the second its wheels were no longer touching the runway and there was thin air below and around and above, and I had never been more alone in my entire life, and all I could think about was things inside of other things, me inside the plane inside the air, Chopin's heart inside a jar inside a brick wall inside Poland, and the baby inside you inside my brain? From that moment on, all I did was come back to you.

When I told you the heart plan, after the initial 'whys', you had googled, 'where is Chopin buried' and the internet had told you he was buried in Paris. 'Look,' you had said, 'he's in Paris. You can take the train. You could go for the day.' And I'd had to explain to you – and in explaining it noticed the weirdness of it all over again – that, yes, Chopin was buried in Paris, but his heart, his literal heart, was in Warsaw. Yet again, you were forced to ask *why*.

The first answer I gave was that Chopin, on his deathbed, was seized by a patriotic frenzy, and expressed the wish that wherever his body ended up, his heart be returned to his homeland. In this version, the request is born of love for his country. I imagine a kind of homesickness in Chopin's bones, growing more intense the closer he came to death. A sense of never being able to sit comfortably; fidgeting, itching for home, for Poland, a country whose name in English gets tangled in my brain with his own – Poland, Chopin, Cho-Poland – and which in Polish sounds like music, a kind of dance: Polska, polka. 'Did Chopin ever write a polka', I google, and learn that the Polka in C minor, posthumously attributed to Chopin, could have been written by his pupil Charlotte de Rothschild. I fall down a rabbit hole of internet searches; I listen to the polka on repeat, trying to recognise Chopin in it, as though I would be the one, finally, to crack the case. Hours later I emerge, unsure what, if anything, I was looking for.

A second answer: Chopin, in his final weeks, developed a terrible fear of being buried alive. As his illness worsened, the fear increased until he was dreaming about it, afraid even to shut his eyes. How awful, he thought, to be trapped inside something like that, to be cut off from the whole world, suspended in the dark and hammering to get out, never knowing whether anyone was there. ('This has nothing to do with the baby, by the way,' I told you.) To ensure he wouldn't wake up underground, Chopin requested that his heart be taken from his body before he was buried. And so when he died, his sister, Ludwika Jędrzejewicz, removed his heart and placed it in a jar of cognac. She smuggled it, under her cloak, back to Warsaw, where it was eventually interred at the Holy Cross church on Krakowskie Przedmieście.

The third answer is that Ludwika Jędrzejewicz was crazy.

*

In the taxi from Warsaw airport, the radio was playing a Polish pop song. I tried and failed to get a sense of the meaning of the words; I noticed – guessed – that it was in G major; I imagined it was a love song, because most songs are. When the driver turned it off, what was left was the hum of the engine, possibly F sharp. 'Oh,' I said, 'you can turn it back on.' I mimed twisting a dial, as though that was still how radios worked, but by then we were drawing up outside my hotel and the driver was saying something in Polish, which I guessed was, 'You are here.' I looked out of the window: I was there. I had been so preoccupied with the music that I'd barely noticed the city.

In the hotel lobby, there was a sculpture: a large glass vase, and inside it, neon strands twisting like branches, brittle. The light emitted a faint, persistent buzz, as though it was trying to say something: *psst*, it said, *psst, psst, over here*. It sounded as though an insect were trapped inside the glass, frantic wings strumming the surface.

I checked in. I filled out the form with my name and address. Behind me, I could hear the neon whispering.

'Are you here for work, or for a vacation?' the man behind the desk asked.

'Work,' I said.

'Work' being shorthand for: I am working something out. 'Work' meaning: I am working on myself. 'Work' as in: I am freaking out, my wife is pregnant, and by focusing on a very specific task like this one, however peculiar and ostensibly pointless, I am hoping to reassure myself that I can handle all of this and God I hope it works.

In my room, I changed my shoes, grabbed the guidebook I had bought at the airport. I took out my phone to text you – *Safely arrived!* – and slid it back into my pocket before I could think too much about *new arrivals* again. Then I hurried to leave. I did not pause to shower, or to lie on my back on the bed and stare at the high ceiling above it. I did not listen to the *psst, psst* of the neon light in the lobby as I passed it, again, to step into a valve of the revolving door. I emerged from the hotel onto the bright street, and I began to walk through Warsaw, towards Chopin's heart.

I listened out for it more than I looked, more than I felt the cobbles underfoot or the hot light on my face: Chopin's heartbeat in the footsteps of passers-by, tourists and tour guides, a woman hand in hand with a little girl, a man holding up a bunch of big red heart-shaped helium balloons in a square next to a boy selling bread rolls, which were nestled together on a trolley, each one a little heart, plump and primed. There was a spring in my step, my pulse rising. *Take heart!* I thought, as I walked and walked and snippets of conversation in Polish floated past me and I understood nothing but believed with all my heart that I was nearing Chopin's heart, was being drawn nearer to it, by it.

I turned down an alley: sunlit buildings chequered with dark doorways like piano keys. A woman in one of the houses was singing. A child laughed. A car horn sounded.

The guidebook said I was just under a mile away from where I was meant to be.

The guidebook said the buildings I was standing next to had all been destroyed in the Second World War and then reconstructed based on cityscapes by the eighteenth-century Italian painter Bernardo Bellotto. I thought of you saying the baby would be a 'new start' and how that had terrified me: how I had tried to find the words to tell you I didn't want anything to change, I loved you as you were, I loved everything as it was. I watched your stomach round, listened to your commentary each morning on how hard it was to do up your jeans, and then I bought you different jeans. My own stomach was the same as ever: unextended, empty. I didn't know what alarmed me more: how fast everything was happening, or that nothing was happening to me.

I made a mental note to tell you about the reconstruction of Old Warsaw, how things could be entirely new and still look exactly the same.

The guidebook said that in many cases, only the fronts of the destroyed buildings had been restored. Inside, they were modern: high ceilings; clean lines. A facade of continuity. Enormous change behind the scenes. The author of the guidebook suggested this was the best of both worlds.

The jar of Chopin's heart in cognac didn't have a fixed abode until thirty years after his death. My internet searches revealed no information about where it was in those three decades. I imagined it gathering dust at the back of a cupboard, beside the kinds of things that are put away and forgotten: pickled lemons, pasta sauce, supermarket panettone from several Christmases ago. Or perhaps it wasn't hidden at all. I pictured the heart wandering, half-lost like

I was, through the streets of Warsaw, searching for a place to end up.

In 1879, after years of nowhere-ness, it found a home in the Holy Cross church, where it was placed behind a stone bust of Chopin's face and the words, *'Gdzie skarb twój, tam i serce twoje,'* taken from the Book of Matthew: 'Where your treasure is, there your heart will be also.' This is pleasing for two reasons. The first is that when I initially read it, I thought it was saying that Chopin's heart *is* treasure, though on reflection that's not right. The second is that it's not clear who the 'you' is: it could mean Chopin himself, could mean that Poland is his treasure and that his heart is with Poland (it probably does mean this but what if it doesn't?); it could mean *me*: where *my* treasure is, there will *my* heart be also. In which case: is *my* treasure Chopin's heart, or is Chopin's heart *my* heart?

And then, eventually, the Nazis took it. In occupied Poland, performances of Chopin's music were prohibited. The statue of Chopin in Warsaw's Łazienki Park was blown up. Chopin's heart, planted deep inside the Holy Cross church, was removed by Nazi officials. It was held by a high-ranking SS commander called Erich von dem Bach-Zelewski, who professed to love Chopin, who was only doing what was best, for Chopin and for everyone, for safekeeping.

When the heart was returned to the church, it was ninety-six years since Chopin had died. Flags lined the route the heart took. People gathered to throw flowers in its path.

*

By the time I found the Holy Cross church I was overheated from the walk, sweaty and a little dusty. There had been no flags to show me where to go, no garlands; the map bore no relation at all to what I could see around me. It had taken me three times as long as it should.

The air in the church was thickly cool, and my skin prickled. A choir was rehearsing. Everywhere: the echoey chill of the singers' voices. And it was as though the space was full of water; as though I was submerged in a swimming pool. It was hard to move forwards, but hard, too, to go back. I waded down the steps towards the central aisle, and the music was so persistent I felt as though I couldn't see: not even the great gleaming altar, or the white walls or the dark pews or the shadows everywhere. I blinked. I took a breath.

I didn't recognise what they were singing: it swelled and ebbed away and then interrupted itself, starting all over again. The sound was crisp. It seemed to have edges, like the fine glass of a neon tube. And I wished they would stop singing, wished they would clamp their lips together and cut the sound off mid-flow. Because they were drowning out the real music; they were making it impossible to hear what I had come all that way to hear.

I found the heart – or rather, the pillar in which the heart was embedded – exactly as I had seen it in pictures: dark-grey stone against light-grey stone, and in neat black lettering, as though none of this was strange:

TU SPOCZYWA SERCE

FRYDERYKA

CHOPINA

HERE RESTS THE HEART

OF

FREDERICK CHOPIN

I wanted to reach up and pick the letters off the wall. I wanted to peel them away from the stone one by one and tuck them into the back pocket of my jeans. I didn't like the phrase 'Here rests the heart'. I didn't like the word 'rests'. I wanted to cross out the word 'rests' and replace it, in permanent marker scrawled above, with 'beats'. Here beats the heart of Frederick Chopin. I pressed a hand against my own heart and thought, *Here beats the heart of me.*

If only the choir would stop singing, I thought, *I would hear it. My heart. Chopin's heart.*

At the hospital, the sonographer doing your ultrasound seemed unimpressed by the magic she was performing. She slid the probe over your domed stomach, and from a machine resting on the trolley by the bed, the sound of the baby's heart blared: rubbery, persistent, as though someone was massaging two balloons together.

'It sounds like balloons,' I said.

You said, 'It sounds like soldiers marching,' and then I

heard it that way, too: hundreds of footsteps in time, a little too fast to be sanguine, rushing towards something or fleeing something else.

There was an army marching, invisibly, behind the smooth wall of your skin. You seemed transformed, as the heartbeat continued to applaud us from the monitor, from a person into a surface, flattened and surprised, as strange and upside down as a foetus. You didn't notice whatever the look on my face was.

'It's a girl,' the doctor said.

When it was over, you took fistfuls of tissues to wipe the gel from your stomach.

Later, when we got home, you were jubilant, as though you'd won a prize, and I retreated into the bedroom. I listened to Chopin's Nocturne in E flat major Op. 9, No. 2. I listened to the *Raindrop Prelude* (Op. 28, No. 15). I looked up videos of people playing Chopin online: beginners hesitantly picking out the melodies; virtuosos whose fingers seemed not to touch the keys. I listened to his Polonaise No. 6 in A flat on YouTube and read the comments underneath:

> *I wish Chopin had a youtube channel and uploaded new music every week.*
>
> *This song has a huge problem! It ends!!*
>
> *Is polonaise an instrument.*

I thought: *I don't want to lose you. I don't want to lose you. I don't want to lose you.*

When the Polonaise ended, I heard water rushing: you were running a bath.

I pressed my face against the cold stone between me and Chopin's heart. The folds of my ear flattened; my cheek cooled. I pushed away the phrase 'Here rests the heart'. Also the phrase: *Like getting blood from a stone.* Also the phrase: *I don't want to lose you.* I pushed away the sound of the choir singing, and the thought of your sleeping, oblivious face, and the thought of your expressionless stomach, bulging like an eyelid.

And what I heard was silence. What I heard was the sound of sedate, unmoveable stone; particles fixed in hard, grainy order. Nothing. I heard nothing at all.

Until, that is, I heard something.

I heard a low, persistent buzz: repetitive, insistent, pulsing. I felt certain I could feel it, too, tickling the pads of my fingers, reaching all the way down my back: the stone resonant, coming to life, purring like a cat.

I cut my breath off in my throat. I held on tighter, as though my life depended on it. The buzzing continued, on-off-on-off, slow.

Somebody nearby hissed at me. I tried to ignore it. I wanted to listen. A man approached and murmured, *'Twój telefon dzwoni.'*

I shook my head, tried to indicate I was busy.

'Twój telefon,' he said again, more forcefully. He pointed at me. He lifted a hand to the side of his face and extended the little finger and thumb. *'Twój telefon.'*

I closed my eyes, listened for one more second, then admitted I knew what he meant.

My phone was still ringing when I slid it out of the back pocket of my jeans, its face a luminous blue and your name flashing on the screen. Then it stopped, and the phone said *(2) missed calls.* Both were from you. I looked up to thank the man, though what I felt was more like boiling rage – it was his fault, after all, that I could no longer feel what I had been feeling before – but he was gone. I let myself lean against the pillar and breathed out. I called you back. The phone played a rippling sound as it waited for you to answer.

It was a case, I knew, of listening very carefully, as I had been ever since I'd arrived. *Keep your eyes peeled* was the phrase I had in mind, and what I was doing was peeling my ears and keeping them that way: open, expectant, exposed. A word might appear in a Polish sentence – *telefon* – that was recognisable. The neon might have a message to deliver. The stone might start to vibrate.

'Hi,' you said. 'Hi. Can you hear me?'

'The signal's very bad,' I whispered. 'I'm in a church. The signal's very bad.' A tourist, standing very close, glared at me. She was holding up a camera. I was ruining her shot of Chopin's heart. I waved at her to apologise, and in doing so let go of the pillar, was standing on my own.

'The baby,' you said, and then the phone crackled.

'What? The baby what? Are you all right?'

'Clicked,' you said.

'What?'

'Ticked,' you said.

'What? I can't hear you. The baby what?'

The line cleared.

'Kicked,' you said. 'The baby kicked. She's never done that before.'

'Oh,' I said, 'oh,' and I was thinking about how loud the baby was, suddenly, how urgent and imminent and potent and completely new she was, lurking behind the familiar facade of you. 'I'm coming home now,' I said. 'Hello? Can you hear me? I said I'm coming home.'

'Hello?' you said. 'Can you hear me?'

'Hello?' I said. 'Can you hear me?'

The signal had cut out, and there was nothing on the other end of the line. I listened anyway, to the neon buzz, a quivering crackle. To the sound of things inside of other things, a heart in cognac, an insect trapped in glass. All the love I had for you was tucked neatly inside of me, and inside of you was all your everything, your lungs and blood and bones and spleen and all of your ideas, all of your self and all of what was about to happen to both of us, all of our future, unknowable and unstoppable.

My Long-Distance Girlfriend

We were watching videos of marmosets, my long-distance girlfriend and I, when the president of her country called for a return to national purity. There was my long-distance girlfriend in her bedroom in the top-floor apartment she shared with five other people in an artsy neighbourhood of a small university town in the north of her country, and there I was in the basement room of my godfather's house in Hackney, staring at her face in the corner of my laptop screen and thinking she was almost unacceptably beautiful, and there *she* was, my long-distance girlfriend's president, standing behind a podium at a press conference that was streaming live to several different news sites, announcing a crackdown on traitors, deviants and spies. I arranged the windows on my computer so our three faces appeared side by side beneath the marmosets, as though we were all part of the same conversation.

'For too long,' her president said, 'corrupting forces have moved among us like vipers in the grass, leading our children astray, tainting our proud culture and causing our birth rate to fall.'

The marmosets were eating papaya.

'Am I a viper?' my long-distance girlfriend said. 'I think she's calling me a viper.'

'I think you are a viper,' I said, and then, 'I think we are both vipers.'

The marmosets leapfrogged each other on a narrow branch.

My long-distance girlfriend was called Anna. We had met three months earlier at a conference on the art of political mistranslation. I'd booked a four-day trip to her country to attend the event, which was central to my PhD thesis and at which I was going to give a paper making some slightly overworked links between word-order conventions in several Eastern European languages and notions of political freedom. After meeting Anna I changed my flight to prolong the trip, and then kept changing it for another three weeks. By the time I finally left, Anna and I were entirely embroiled and so everything else that happened felt almost inevitable, though it astonished me at the same time.

Shortly before I left, we had gone to a party at the house of a friend of one of her friends, or not even a friend, she said, more of an acquaintance, someone she'd met at puppetry class. She threw me off with that kind of thing. *Puppetry class.* Casual, serious, as though it was nothing surprising, and every time I wondered whether it was a translation issue, whether I'd simply misunderstood what she'd said, whether the word for puppet in her language was perhaps also slang for something more ordinary, like, I don't know, pottery. And if it wasn't a translation issue, I wondered if it was actually a kind of test, to see how I'd react. Was I someone who could be flustered by a puppet?

It turned out she did mean puppet, and she seemed to mean it genuinely, nothing to do with my reaction, because the acquaintance whose friend was hosting the party had brought one with him and she greeted it like a long-lost relative, air kissing its paper cheeks. Its eyebrows were high arches, reaching up to its hairline; it looked as though it could not believe Anna was really there. I stood back, waiting to be introduced and not sure where to look.

There was one other person I knew at the party, another British academic who had also been at the mistranslation conference and who was staying on to complete a research fellowship at the university; I tried to avoid him as Anna and I made our way towards the kitchen. I hated speaking English when I was with her, and when the academic caught my eye and waved, I smiled enough to be polite and then looked away. There were no glasses or mugs left in the kitchen, so we drank the wine we'd brought straight from the bottle. Later, somebody gave us some sort of vodka cocktail. Even later, shots of something, I'm not sure what, and then we somehow left the party and found our way home. It was March. Snow in the streets was just beginning to melt. It was very cold.

The next morning, we lay in a heap in bed together, her legs on top of mine and her hair tickling my neck. Her breath smelled of alcohol. We were barely awake, scrolling through photos from last night on her phone – it was hard to see them clearly because the screen had shattered, but there was a picture of her posing beside a rocking horse, me looking blurry with my eyes closed, a lot of faces I didn't recognise, several of both of us embracing the surprised puppet – when she found a video. It was of us, propping ourselves up against a sign for a taxi rank on a street I didn't recognise, unsteadily passing a paper cup of something back and forth and both in floods of tears. The video lurched in her hand and sometimes her fingers eclipsed the lens. We looked as though we'd been crying for a while. There were pink blotches on our skin and my nose looked impossibly red. We wailed and wailed and then, in a moment between wailing, she said, 'I love you,' and I began to cry even harder and coughed up, 'I love you,' and then she began to wail again and dropped the phone, so there was just a direct view of a street lamp and a glowing haze of rain and the sound of our voices, quieter.

'I guess that's how my screen got smashed,' she said, thumbing a shard loose.

'I can take it to the repair place by the archives,' I offered. 'I'll be going right by there on Thursday.'

'I don't remember crying last night,' she said. 'Do you?'

I didn't remember.

'I don't remember filming ourselves crying,' I said.

I didn't remember saying I loved her, either, though I felt that I must do. She didn't mention that part, and I wondered if that was because it was inconsequential to her, perhaps obvious or perhaps meaningless, or whether it was too consequential to acknowledge at all.

By Thursday, my PhD supervisor had sent me an extremely stern email demanding I return to the UK to resume my teaching responsibilities, which he'd been covering for me ever since I'd failed to reappear after the mistranslation conference, and I knew I had no choice but to arrange a flight at once if I wanted a career, which I did, or thought I did, so I never fixed her phone.

For a few weeks after I left, Anna still had the internet, more or less. Sites shut down and then re-emerged, briefly, in a way that made it impossible to discern a pattern. Anna's government was already at work protecting its citizens from vipers, though there had been no formal announcement. The way they were going about it was by temporarily shutting down social media and then opening it again at random. Regardless, Anna was persistent about uploading photographs to Instagram at every opportunity: the queues at ATMs when rumours spread of plans to freeze accounts for security checks; missing posters for a man Anna had known loosely through old friends, who had left to get bread one day and never returned; her friends getting ready to go out, painting streaks of grey glitter around their brows and temples. She attended a gathering for those interested in urban beekeeping, and a party that I could tell was meant to be a kind of rally; people had written slogans on their foreheads and chests in lipstick and covered their noses and mouths with strips of cloth made from the country's traditional fabric. Then there was no Instagram.

When I called to ask how she was, I asked about the Instagram outage and she began telling me about clown school, which she had attended for three days the previous year before dropping out.

'It was very uptight,' she said. 'Nobody put a toe out of line.'

I pictured the enormous, upturned toes of clown shoes, nervous and poised. 'Why would you go in the first place?'

'I didn't want to go through life not knowing what it's like to be utterly abject.'

'That's a very interesting way of putting it,' I said, because she had used a specific word-order pattern in her language that I had written about in the second chapter of my thesis.

'I wanted to know,' she said, 'what it is like to be utterly abject.'

'And then when you knew, you dropped out.'

'No, it was that I realised clowns aren't abject after all. They're actually very manipulative.'

I had the constant urge to ask her the serious questions, of course, about her missing friend and the frozen bank accounts and all the rest, but she had a way of repelling topics she didn't want to talk about. She would say only, 'It's very bad,' or 'It's getting very bad,' and then would revert to anecdotes about clowns, or bees. We were sort of killing time, just talking and talking because whenever we weren't talking it felt hollow, too quiet. I was twitchy, distracted, barely able to speak even to my godfather, who was letting me live with him for free while I was finishing up my PhD in return for, in his words, 'being young and happy in his house'. He tried to give me space. He peered into my basement bedroom sporadically, trying not to glance too obviously at my computer screen, offering me coffee, cigarettes, some sort of herbal tea he claimed would help with anxiety. It was sort of a joke between us that he would kick me out or start charging rent because I wasn't happy enough, but there was part of me that felt genuinely bad about not keeping up my end of the bargain.

'People are scared,' Anna said, when pushed.

'I'm not unhappy,' I said to my godfather.

My departure from Anna's country happened at speed and inelegantly, and there wasn't really time to say any of the things I wanted to say.

The university travel agent was unnervingly prompt and within twenty-four hours of my supervisor's email, my journey home was booked for later that same day. There was limited availability at such short notice, they said, so it involved a bus to the border and a flight from the neighbouring country's second-largest airport. I didn't have much to do to get ready but still I felt slightly panicked, as though I was undergoing some sort of emergency. I packed my clothes and checked I had my passport and made coffee and called my godfather to let him know what was going on, and said goodbye to Anna's housemates, including the two goldfish they kept in the sitting room and in whom I'd already become quite invested, giving them personalities and little backstories about the vicissitudes of their relationship in the bowl, believing I'd have longer to spend with them.

I took photographs of the notes I'd written by hand in the reading room at the national archives, which were three blocks from Anna's house. I had justified extending my stay in the country by the presence of these archives, declaring they were indispensable to my thesis, but I'd spent only a few hours there. In part this was because I was giving all my time to Anna and in part this was because I felt after spending time with her, I now understood things I hadn't before, about the language and the country and the things the people of this country had written about the country in the language of the country; I could not possibly understand anything better than I did, then, and nothing the archives held could really help.

She got back from work just as I was carrying my bags down from her room upstairs. She jumped at the sight of me and then laughed at having been surprised and then she leant forwards to kiss me. She seemed more anxious than usual to touch me. She ran her hands down my forearms, fluttered her fingers on my knuckles.

'So you're leaving?' she said, which annoyed me, and I didn't know how to reply.

It wasn't that I hadn't thought about this exact moment; I had been imagining our parting since we'd first met, wondering about it and worrying about it and wanting to know what Anna thought, how Anna was thinking any of this might go. I'd known that falling in love with someone while attending a conference on political mistranslation was both a cliché and a logistical nightmare. My mind had returned to it over and over, trying to see how it would work, how things would go, what a future might look like in which I somehow never had to leave. I'd pictured high summer, the two of us standing in the shade somewhere elegant in the city I had yet to discover. I'd pictured a scenario in which my supervisor was incredibly supportive, saying things like, 'Love is the greatest form of research!' and 'Nothing is more important than the discovery of a kindred human spirit!' though in reality he was a reserved and somewhat arch person who never proclaimed about anything. I'd pictured a scenario in which we had enough time – for what, I didn't know – just enough time to figure out everything else. Like, for example, whether we had meant it when we bawled at the taxi rank and said we loved each other, whether both of us had meant it or just one of us or neither.

And then there was no time at all – and for some reason what I said was, 'See you later,' which we both realised was deeply hurtful, though I couldn't pinpoint why.

I didn't cry on the bus to the border, but when we got into the neighbouring country and all the other passengers cheered as though we had staged a great escape, I couldn't help it. And when I got home to my godfather's basement, I felt as though anything at all could tip me over into tears: Post-it notes I had written before I left for the conference reminding me of things I needed to do when I got back, which seemed like missives from a different person entirely; the smell of the whole house, of my godfather, domestic and unchanged; my thesis, a word file on my computer saved as thesisyear3draft9.docx, a sprawling mass of words, as though I meant it, as though I knew what I wanted to say, when in reality I had fallen into academia through a lack of imagination, BA, MA, PhD and at no point had I thought to myself, yes, this is what I want, I want to be an expert on the implications of word order in certain Eastern European languages, this is who I want to be, and yet there I was, doing it, being it, not even remotely on purpose.

On FaceTime, Anna fell asleep – it was an hour ahead where she was, dawn an hour closer for her – and I froze, feeling that if I moved I might somehow wake her. We'd been talking, murmuring, not talking, staring for hours. Her phone slid out of her hand so the view was of half her forehead and the wall behind her. I could hear her breathing, and, faintly, the sounds of traffic outside on her street; about half an hour later, there was the shuffling and muffled laughter of her flatmates coming home from a bar; occasionally her dog grunted and snuffled in his sleep. If I'd closed my eyes, I would have been back there, with her, in her apartment. I'd have been able to smell the leathery, liquorice scent of her dog's fur, and the cigarette smoke curling under her bedroom door from the sitting room where the others would gather. I would have been able to turn my head and see her full face again, fuzzy in the darkness. I thought I could remember everything, the smells and the feel of being beside her, if I wanted to. I didn't close my eyes. The section of her forehead on the screen looked alien, like it belonged to someone or something else entirely. It could have been a buttock, or a knee. It could have been a pale, barren hill. I lay there, hardly breathing, waiting for enough time to pass that I too would fall asleep, or she would wake up.

When we met at the conference, she'd been wearing a tag with somebody else's name on it. I was discombobulated on that first day, having only landed the previous night, and I was nervous because I was due to present my paper that afternoon. There were several people from my department at the conference, because there had been some sort of unusual funding situation that meant the university needed to spend money earmarked for travel before the tax year ended. I felt an almost pathological need to avoid anyone I knew. I could embarrass myself in front of strangers, I could tolerate that, but not in front of all these people from home. When Anna came up to me by the buffet lunch table and held out her hand and introduced herself by a name that wasn't the one on her badge, I kept talking to her to get out of talking to anyone else.

'Oh,' she said, fiddling with the badge, 'that's my friend. She couldn't come and since I don't know anything about political mistranslation, I thought I would see what it was like.'

'Are you not an academic?' I asked, which sounded hopelessly naive, maybe also judgemental.

She looked extremely serious. 'I am not an academic,' she said.

Later I learned that she worked as a cashier in a bank, though it was not information she offered freely. I had the impression she thought it made her seem less interesting.

The people I knew from home seemed to glide through the conference, laughing outside the breakout rooms and talking knowingly about local bars that were worth going to, a great little place just on the corner of somewhere I hadn't heard of. At breakfast in the hotel where we were all staying they had seemed already familiar with the menu, advising each other and me on what to order. I experienced a nauseous kind of envy that they could translate themselves so easily, and felt myself to be obvious by comparison, unsophisticated and unprepared, though I spoke the language as well as any of them and was just as capable of googling where was good to go out. In the first coffee break, I looked up the bars they had mentioned online, scrolling through photos of strangers who had tagged themselves there. Then, in front of the buffet lunch, I asked Anna, who at that point was just a stranger wearing someone else's name badge, what was good to eat.

'Oh,' she said, 'none of this, I shouldn't think. I don't know what any of it is.'

I was always terrified of not knowing things, of being shown up, but when Anna didn't know things she made it seem sophisticated.

On the final night of the conference, the people from home told me they were going to a club. I had found my feet by then, got my paper out of the way, and I knew that once I got back to the basement of my godfather's house, I would probably wish I had gone with them.

Something about being there at the conference reminded me of being much younger than I was; there was an adolescent tension to the group dynamics, about who sat next to whom, about who was going out each night and who wasn't. People were sending lots of messages on group chats, complaining about their hangovers, crying-laughing emojis. I'd never once detected this kind of giddiness from my colleagues when we were in London. It was as though people at the political mistranslation conference were on holiday from their normal personalities. I dithered for three hours about the club before deciding I should go.

I wore the one nice outfit I'd brought with me, short sleeves even though it was too cold and shoes with no grip that made crossing the cobbles impossible. I felt childish, like I didn't know how to be in my body. I was suddenly and embarrassingly homesick, though we were due to fly back the next day: missing my godfather, missing London, missing being able to speak without thinking, to say whatever, without having to doubt myself or question whether I was expressing what I wanted to express. The night ahead seemed very long, with so much potential for language, so many words to say or missay, and who would I say them to? That sort of thing.

Then I went into the club, which was dark and smelled damp and was playing music that seemed hard to dance to, though people were dancing, and Anna was there and I thought, as I had on the first day at lunch, that if I stuck with her I'd make more sense to myself.

It should have come as no surprise, the purity thing, the vipers. I had received extensive briefing notes from the university about the country's politics, its sudden shift from liberal democracy to autocracy under a capricious leader, its murky surveillance and its oppressive laws, though in fact all of this was part of my research and I had visited the capital city several times and felt I knew more about it all than whoever had written the briefing. My supervisor, who had young children and so was not travelling to the conference, told me to wait a moment after the department meeting and then said,

'You must be careful when you get there.' I said I would, of course. 'No,' he said, 'I mean *you*. Specifically, you should be careful.' At the time I'd felt uneasy but once I'd arrived and met Anna and her friends, saw how confident they were, how they dressed and held hands when they wanted to, and once, even, saw her two male friends kiss each other in the street – it seemed that the severity of things had been overstated. Anna never kissed me in public, but that could have just been a personal choice. She seemed free – infinitely freer than I felt, in any case – and I wanted to feel that way too.

But the viper thing had unnerved her. She refused to say how she really felt, yet she would nonetheless loop round to vipers in conversations that were not about vipers, and she began to talk about the president, too, about the way the press reported on the president's shoes and nail polish and new hairstyles and how the president was a wonderful mother and how the president had said something witty and rude about another country's leader, but never on what the president was actually doing to people's lives and I didn't know, increasingly I didn't know, what she wanted me to say in return.

'It's bad,' she said, and then she talked about urban bee-keeping for a while, then told me the story about clown school again, and in a different kind of person this would have been annoying, the way her randomness had a certain defensive edge, almost artificial, and the repetitiveness of her stories, too, but it wasn't annoying when she did it. I was happy to talk about clown school again.

*

'You could come here,' I said. 'You could come here and we could get married.' I realised when I said it that I had deliberately not thought about it in advance, that any time my mind had veered in that direction I had steered it somewhere else, so the words came as a surprise to me, too, completely new information. I seemed to be more shocked than she was because she said, 'Yes,' before I'd had time to state all the reasons why she probably wouldn't want to.

'Yes,' she said, 'I want that.' And then she carried on talking, even before I'd had a chance to say, 'Wow,' or 'Great,' or 'Really?' She was talking about arrangements, about her apartment and her job at the bank and her dog and the difficulties, now, with even paying for a flight because of issues with her currency—

'It would be here, with my godfather,' I said, before she could finish. 'He plays the ukulele and smokes weed in his greenhouse. It's kind of boring. I'm worried you won't like it.'

'I like everything,' she said, and that was true, she did; if that was my reason for not marrying her, it was a bad one. 'I'm never bored,' she said. That was true too.

I paid for her flight with my credit card while my godfather hovered behind me asking questions about logistics – but how will she get to the airport, but will she have enough time to change planes – to which I just said, 'I don't know, I don't know,' and typed out the numbers as fast as I could, because I realised only then that Anna had been waiting and waiting for me to do this; I had been thinking we were watching marmosets together or making jokes about her friends or talking about urban bees, but actually what we had been doing was waiting for me to tell her to come.

'How well do you really know this person?' my godfather asked. 'You were in the same country for what, three weeks?'

'Three and a half weeks,' I said.

'I just worry,' he said. I could see he was choosing his words carefully. 'I just worry that you're imagining this person can solve things that, maybe, you have to solve yourself.' He was referring to, I assumed, his perception that I was not particularly happy in my life.

I emailed Anna the details, messaged to say I'd be waiting at the airport, and she was so busy packing up her life and saying goodbye to everyone and finding a home for her dog that she didn't have time to talk, just sent a single red heart that pulsed on the screen.

I looked around at my godfather's basement and tried to imagine her in it. There were framed photos on the windowsill of my godfather's school friends, some of whom had died, all of whom looked like they came not just from a different country and time to Anna, but an entirely different genre of life. In a box under the bed there were trinkets from my childhood I'd found myself unable to leave behind when I moved to London – pebbles and feathers and a little wooden bull my father had brought back from a work trip to Madrid – and suddenly its presence felt mortifying, as though Anna might arrive and discover it and realise who I was. I wasn't sure what I was scared she'd find out, exactly, but I was scared she'd find me out nonetheless.

On the desk were all my books, my embarrassing books all

about how to understand the language she spoke, that she and I spoke to each other. There were my folders of notes; there was my laptop; there was, still, the little packet of documents I'd had to prepare in order to travel to her country for the conference: my passport, insurance documents, visa. I called her.

'What?' She was out of breath. I imagined her the way I had been when I found out I was leaving, overburdened and over-caffeinated.

'Wait,' I said, 'wait, you need a visa. I didn't even think about it but you need a visa before you can come.'

'I know,' she said. 'I applied for it the day that you left. It's valid for 123 more days.'

The evening before Anna came, the news reported a cloud of Saharan dust was being blown across Europe, approaching the UK, and the next day I woke up to find everything coated in orange sand: it collected in the grooves on top of my godfather's bins and made the tiled front path slippery. I wondered how it would come up in conversation: 'Welcome, darling, to this place that is not normally covered in red dust.' Perhaps she wouldn't even notice it. Perhaps her country had been covered in red dust too.

When she appeared in the arrivals hall, wheeling a case behind her that kept tipping to one side, she looked so exactly like herself and so entirely out of place that for a second I couldn't breathe. My long-distance girlfriend, right there, at close range. I raised a hand to wave to her but she'd already seen me, was breaking into a run, heaving the lopsided luggage after her.

My long-distance girlfriend, ducking under the barrier.

My long-distance girlfriend, larger than I had anticipated, taller and more embodied, and I could even smell her skin and her detergent, which was a kind not sold in the UK: minty and sharp.

My long-distance girlfriend, astonishing to me in her odours and textures and voice, like her own kind of Saharan dust, unimaginable over FaceTime and, I realised, oddly forgettable, since surely I had known them, surely I had loved them when she and I had been together in her country.

When she put a hand on my cheek and moved her face towards mine, I tensed, just for a second, before our lips touched, and I felt the same in her, a kind of reticence I'd never previously observed, reluctance even. We kissed. There was no distance, nothing at all, between us.

And this was before we discovered that I didn't earn enough money for her to be eligible for a spousal visa, and this was before we began the work of arguing with the Home Office, and this was before, too, she briefly had to go back to her country and then apply to return from there and we were terrified, really terrified that time, about what was going to happen. It was before I finished my PhD and got a job in a field utterly unrelated to anything to do with her country or the ways in which the word-order conventions in certain Eastern European languages related or did not relate to notions of political freedom. It was before we found a home for ourselves and a rhythm and a kind of solidness together, before I learned that worrying about randomness, thinking, *But this is only this way because this happened and then this happened to happen,* was an empty pursuit, no more meaningful than anything else.

It did not matter that I did not really know Anna, but I didn't know that yet, which is the kind of garbled sentence she would get frustrated with me for using in her early days of learning English – 'Do you not want me to understand you?' – and so better to say: it mattered that I knew her, but I didn't know that yet.

What I was thinking about, kissing Anna in the arrivals hall with the speakers announcing other flights and the squeaks of trolley wheels around us and people streaming through the gates, was that moment at the end of the night when the lights come up in a club and everyone is revealed, sweaty and flushed and ordinary-looking, though moments before it had been all shimmer and strangeness and vibration, and you're left thinking, *Wait, was this all it was the whole time, just us in our bodies in a room? Was it only ever us, together, like this?* You have to fumble your way out into the night, where the world carries on just as it did before, traffic passing on the road. You have to hold hands with the person you are with, and then you have to find your way home.

The Good Time

By then, I was used to getting emails from my dead friend Sam. They'd started a year or so after his funeral. 'I thought you would appreciate this one,' the first subject line had read, and in the body of the message there was a link to a discount-sunglasses site. Afterwards there had been a little flurry of texts between my friends, who had all received the same message, everyone reassuring everyone else it was some sort of spam, or hack, or bot (we didn't really understand any of those words) and telling each other not to click on the link. We had begun to drift apart by then. The email from Sam had the effect of reuniting us briefly. We all said we should block his address and then resumed not talking.

But I couldn't bring myself to block Sam. When another message arrived – 'Check this out, I think you'll like it' – I opened it and was directed to a website selling weight-loss pills. 'Thought of you when I saw this,' the emails said, or 'I knew you'd want to see this.' I opened them with such eagerness and stared at them for so long that my computer started labelling the emails with little stars to show they were important. This went on for years, and over time the subject lines got longer and more unwieldy, and more personal too, because they included the first half of my email address, which was my name and year of birth.

'JessicaBroder82, you are the type of dude that I will like to be with in my vicinity,' Sam wrote, sending a link to a dating site. 'JessicaBroder82, my name is Mrs Elizabeth Patten,' Sam wrote, 'and I am a dying, sick woman, who wants to donate $2,000,000 United States dollars to you for charity work worldwide.' My old friends and I no longer discussed the emails, or anything else for that matter. So it was only Sam, out of all of them, who stayed in touch.

And then there was another email, with a rambling subject line like all the others – 'JessicaBroder82, all the time you have spent alone can be enjoyed in the company of a lady that is pleased to be with you' – except that in place of a link to buy knock-off trainers or Viagra or a mail-order bride, it sent me instead, via a jerky series of redirects, to a website for a hotel in Cumbria called The Swan. Which might not have been so strange, were it not for the fact that this was the hotel that Sam had bought in his late twenties with money from an unexpected inheritance. It had sold to a corporation running care homes after his death and now, I learned from this email, it was a hotel again.

I clicked through pages on the website, noting how little the place seemed to have changed: the same dark facade and stained-glass panels around the main entrance, the rooms all painted in dim, vaguely natural colours, with the kind of seagrass carpets that were painful underfoot. The restaurant had been refurbished; there were more tables now, and the menu was, for some reason, mostly Italian food. There was an 'About the Owners' section, which contained a photo of two smiling, middle-aged women and no mention of Sam. Of course there was no mention of Sam. Sam was a dead man who no longer owned the hotel.

I opened the old group chat my friends and I had once used daily. The last message was from five years earlier, when someone had posted a photograph of us all from five years before that. Sam was in the picture. We were all at The Swan.

Hi everyone, I wrote and pressed send.

It's Jess, I said, in case they had deleted my number.

Have you seen that The Swan is open again, I wrote.

We should go back and see the place, I wrote.

If anyone is interested, I wrote. Then I waited for them to write back.

We had all said Sam was deranged when he quit his job as a product development co-ordinator in London and bought a hotel in a small village called Ashby-on-Lune in Cumbria. It felt like the loving thing to do, to say he was mad and would lose all his money and come crawling back to sleep on our sofas. That was the kind of friends we were, had always been. We weren't particularly nice to each other, but it felt like we were being nice all the same. *Ashby-on-Lunacy,* joked the group chat. *InSAMity.* It was a way of saying he was brave. It was a way of saying we all wished we could be more like him.

Sam went ahead and bought the place, though it was near derelict and in the middle of nowhere. He spent his inheritance from his estranged father, who had died with no warning the previous year, and took out a substantial bank loan on the project. It was beautiful by the time he was done, really beautiful, and it was featured in the weekend supplements of all the major papers at one time or another. The restaurant did hog roasts on Friday nights and had a whole thing about nose-to-tail eating, which made me feel faintly queasy but was extremely fashionable then. The Swan became the kind of place where people posted pictures of their breakfast on the internet: bacon from local pigs and eggs laid in the farm down the road. Guests took selfies of themselves in the giant bay windows beside curtains in neutral linen, a view of the hills behind them. It was popular with city types who liked the idea of the countryside more than the reality of it, and who called the little forty-minute walk along the disused railway line below the hotel a 'hike'.

Sam loved it. Sam was having the time of his life.

The rest of us, Sam's friends, would drive up on Friday afternoons after work and stay for the weekend, occupying a position somewhere between guests and staff: we enjoyed the rooms and facilities but also meandered behind the scenes, loaded trays of dirty plates into the big industrial dishwasher and sliced sourdough during the breakfast rush. I became skilled at frothing milk for coffees, even almond milk, which was trickier. We ate the little packets of biscuits laid out by the kettles in our rooms, and then helped ourselves to more from the enormous box full of the little packets, which was stored in a disused lift. We sometimes checked in guests or answered their queries, feeling a need to demonstrate that we were earning our keep.

In the evenings, we would sit by the fire after the last guests had gone to bed, drinking wine that Sam got discounted from his supplier and playing a game we called 'Rock Paper Anything', which was a version of Rock Paper Scissors, but instead of rock or paper or scissors, you could play whatever you liked. You counted to three while bouncing your fists, and then mimed what your *anything* was to the best of your ability, and then normally had to explain, and then we would sit around and discuss what should win. You could play rock versus scissors. You could play a helicopter versus the devil. You could play a bad egg versus the ennui experienced while unpacking your suitcase upon returning home from holiday. You could play paper if you wanted. It never made any sense. We found it so funny.

I think I had the feeling, even then, that this was a uniquely good time we were having. We were school friends who had stayed close through our twenties; we were old enough to have abandoned uncertainties, but none of us yet had the kinds of responsibilities that would curtail our freedom: children, extremely important positions at work. We were in our early thirties and would not have been able to afford to stay in Sam's hotel if it hadn't been Sam's. I had the giddy, delighted sense that we were getting away with something. We liked each other's company so much, the group of us. We enjoyed ourselves so much.

Four years after he bought the hotel, Sam died suddenly and horribly. It felt unfair to meet up without him, as though we were leaving him out on purpose, so after that we didn't meet up at all.

*

The drive up was longer than I remembered. I left work early but it was nearly midnight by the time I arrived in Ashby-on-Lune. The lane that led to The Swan was unlit; my headlights glanced off the low, mossy drystone walls that bordered it. The new owners had strung bistro lights around the trees in front of the hotel, so when I turned the final corner it was bright and I realised only then that I was terrified. Part of me had this idea that I'd burst through the doors into the lobby to find Sam and all my friends, as though they had been there all along and nothing had changed. As though I had been the one who had died.

The sound of the gravel in the car park as my tyres churned over was the same as always. The smell of the air when I opened my door – redolent of manure from the nearby farm and yet somehow also sharply clean – was the same. The stone lions by the front steps were the same stone lions, and it should have been no surprise to find it all unchanged because the whole point, the appeal of a place like The Swan, was that it was unchanging. It had been there for centuries and would always be there, ever thus. The point was that it endured.

Heavy front door. Tiled vestibule lined with wellington boots that were for effect only, not to be used. Framed photograph of the building from the late nineteenth century, its staff lined up out front, crisp white aprons. Lobby, which had the most distinctive scent to it – jarring – of whisky and some sort of expensive detergent. Bookshelves stacked with dusty twentieth-century hardbacks bulk-bought at auction. All just the same as before. Reception desk, unmanned at that hour. Low velvet sofas, dim lighting. The fire was still burning, crackling, a charred log at that very moment giving way and disintegrating with a breathy thud. And there were my friends, sitting at the fireside. Just as, it seemed to me, they always had been.

Only three out of a total of nine had replied to my messages, and two were married to each other so only really counted as one response. Others sent apologies – children, work – and some had taken the opportunity to remove themselves from the group. There was a little string of 'has left's following my invitation. Still, four of us seemed like enough for a reunion, and now there they were, the three others, the backs of their heads so instantly familiar I felt dizzy. I must have creaked a floorboard or announced myself in some other way because all at once they turned to look at me.

Alicia and David, the couple, were side by side on the sofa. He was wearing a baseball cap that was covering – I knew this because I had googled him and found his photo on his law firm's website – a bald spot he'd developed in the nine years since I last saw him. She was very unchanged, a little tired-looking but glossy and slick in the way she had always been. When I got close I saw that her face had set itself rigidly against ageing; there was filler in her cheeks and jaw; her forehead had that tell-tale, expressionless stillness. On a chair nearer the fire was Emma, who had been my closest friend of all, closer even than Sam, and who was smiling at me, beaming, as if she were truly delighted to see me. There was a bowl on the table between them with a single olive in it, and a saucer filled with rubbly pits. A bottle of red, nearly empty. Four glasses, three in use and one clean, for me.

'I can't believe it,' Emma said, rising. 'Here you really are.'

I thought of the title of Sam's last email, 'All the time you have spent alone can be enjoyed in the company of a lady that is pleased to be with you,' and felt sure we had done the right thing, had done such a good thing, the four of us, coming back.

Rock Paper Anything. Sam versus Emma. This must have been towards the end, perhaps our penultimate visit to The Swan, because it was hot and we were all out on the terrace drinking caipirinhas that Sam had mixed himself with home-made chilli-infused sugar syrup. There were heatwaves that summer, one after the other, punctuated by storms. It can't have been our last visit because it rained constantly that time, torrentially, so hard in fact that the blood had washed away from Sam's body almost instantly. So, not the last time, but maybe the time before that.

There we all were, tipsy, the sun setting but still visible. It was late but not very late and there were guests milling around. Emma and Sam bounced their fists against their palms three times and then struck their poses. Sam was standing very straight, arms by his side and his face scrunched up into a horrible, puckered scowl. Emma, facing him, was running on the spot, waving at imaginary people and grinning, looking generally manic and distracted and happy, clownish. She mimed pouring drinks. She mimed smoking. She mimed pouring drinks again.

'What are you?' Emma said to Sam.

'I'm the sensation of paralysis when faced with an overwhelming task,' Sam said. 'What are you?'

'I'm you,' Emma said, and she stopped pretend-running-and-waving and drink-pouring. They sat down and waited for us to judge who would win between Sam and the sensation of paralysis when faced with an overwhelming task.

'So the question is, really, whether Sam gets paralysed when he's overwhelmed,' my friend Yasmin said. 'Pretty simple.'

'Easy,' said Sam. 'I never do.' And that was true, I thought, he never did. He was always busy, always doing something. He never seemed to stop. Even in that moment he was refilling people's glasses from the pitcher. 'Which, ironically, means I've lost.'

'No, not necessarily,' said David. 'There's one area of your life where you are undoubtedly paralysed. Completely torpefied. Rooted to the spot.'

'David,' said Alicia, too quickly.

David seemed a little drunker than the rest of us.

'Well, it's true, he is totally torpefied,' David said, and he nodded towards me.

'What?' I said.

'Is torpefied a word?' said Sam.

The whole group was uneasy; it wasn't just me. Perhaps it had been there from the start, or at least from the moment Emma had portrayed Sam, which had never happened before and seemed too personal, against the spirit of things. People were glancing at each other. People were glancing in particular at me. Several of us turned our attention to our glasses. Emma was patting her pockets, pulling out a packet of cigarettes, and when I looked at Sam he seemed calm, unaffected by the ripple of agitation that had passed through the rest of us. But then, was Sam ever really calm? Wasn't that the point in question? He was digging ice out of the ice bucket. He was unsealing a bottle of cachaça. He said, 'You know what, let me get some more limes,' and scurried off inside.

'Was that really necessary?' Emma said to David, when the door had closed behind Sam.

And what I was thinking was that David could be awful when he was drinking, obnoxious and argumentative. I was thinking that Alicia was irritating, too, for making it more awkward than it needed to be by trying to stop David from speaking. And what I wasn't thinking about was why they were looking at me, why they were in any way making this something to do with me, why anything about Sam would have anything to do with me, when it was just a silly game and we were supposed to be enjoying our weekend together, we were supposed to be having a good time.

One of the things I loved about The Swan, one of the many things I loved about The Swan, was how many opportunities it afforded me to watch my friends. There was a mezzanine that looped above the ground-floor lobby, with little nooks by the banisters so that you could settle into an armchair overlooking the comings and goings of the guests and could, for example, observe two of your friends sitting by the fireside talking, looking easy and happy, making each other laugh, and so could feel both part of the moment with them and far enough removed from it to truly appreciate it, too.

And then there was Room 7, which I jokingly called 'my

room'. It was the smallest and shabbiest and so usually unoccupied when we wanted to stay. It only had a single bed, which was fine by me of course, and no bath, but what I loved about it was its sash window that opened out onto the roof of the atrium below. It wasn't a proper balcony or anything like that, there were no safety measures, railings. It was clear you weren't supposed to go out there. But from the roof you could watch the whole terrace unobserved, the clusters of people sitting out in warm weather, the sheep meandering through the fields beyond; the birds. I could watch my friends gather in twos or threes, or cohere in a cluster around a bottle of wine, could overhear them say something along the lines of, 'Where's Jess?', could clear my throat and wait for them to look up and smile.

People sometimes told me that I was too intense about my friends. That I talked too much or too passionately about them, that their lives loomed too large in my own. To those people I just said: what a shame for you that your friends are not as wonderful as mine. Sometimes, normally after drinking, even my friends told me I was too intense about my friends. I considered this an example of the loving meanness we had cultivated between us. Sam was too mad, Alicia too vain, Jess too intense about everyone, that kind of thing. It was how we showed each other love.

I had asked specifically for Room 7 when I made the booking for our reunion, but the night manager claimed she had no record of the request when she checked me in. I'd had to be quite pushy, more forceful than was comfortable for either of us, to get her to fetch me the right key, and once

I was finally in the room I felt so agitated I stayed awake for hours, sitting on the roof, staring out at nothing. It was dark and there was no moon.

'We were surprised when you wrote,' David said, mildly, at breakfast on the first morning of our return. 'We didn't think you'd ever want to come back here.'

He had this habit, had always had this habit, of speaking casually about things he did not feel casual about.

We were sitting in the restaurant, in one of the bay windows with a view of the terrace. There were a few diners hovering at the buffet, spooling fruit compote onto yogurt, shaking granola and nuts out of Kilner jars. Emma and I were eating croissants and sharing a large pot of coffee. A waiter appeared with eggs Benedict for David and an omelette for Alicia. I had the rasping sensation of a hangover, though I'd only had a single glass of wine the night before. It was the sleeplessness, I supposed. None of us were saying much.

Emma and I had come down that morning both wearing the same green jumper, which had been commented on first by the two of us, and then by Alicia when she appeared and then David when he did, and then even the waiter had made a joke about not getting the memo. As we waited for more coffee to arrive, Alicia had returned to it, had made the joke again, in a way that made it clear we didn't know what else to talk about.

'We thought you'd never want to set foot in this place again,' said David.

'I know what you mean,' I said. 'The risk that seeing it now, different, might ruin all the happy memories.'

David moved his head back as though he were dodging something thrown too close to his face. Alicia, too, looked affronted, her stiff face stiffening, her mouth open around a forkful of egg.

'How's work been, Jess?' Emma said. 'Are you still at the museum?'

It took me a moment to register what she was talking about, which was a job I'd had all those years ago, writing newsletters for a small museum in south-east London. I had quit around the time of the funeral and moved away to the town where my father lived, working first for an estate agent and then for a publisher of medical journals. The thought of myself as Emma suggested I might be, frozen in the life I'd had when we'd been real friends, struck me as very sad. Imagine if nothing else had changed after Sam died. Same flat, same neighbours, same London, same job and my friends all gone, my very best friends all gone. It would have been too much to bear. Had already been too much, and would have been even more.

'There was a risk it would spoil the happy memories,' I said again. They must have misheard or misunderstood me when I answered David before, the way they were reacting. 'But it hasn't been like that, has it? The hotel is really very similar. My room even feels the same; it's like they used the same bed-linen supplier or something. And you'd never know about its care-home years, to look at it. Sam would be so relieved, don't you think? And proud that his legacy lives on.'

Even Emma, now, was looking awkward. Everyone was looking awkward. We looked away from each other, all of us turning our heads to look out of the window, at the hills and the fields and, closer still, the terrace, which is where Sam had landed.

'Of course,' I said quickly, 'there are some awful memories too.'

There was a long silence, then Alicia said, 'I can't believe that after all this time, you two came down in matching jumpers.'

Emma and I had been close for ever, we used to say, though really for ever meant from the first day of secondary school, when we had been put together at the same table because our surnames began with the same letter. She was one of those people who are so easy in their own skin that being around them was easy, too. Even through adolescence, when the rest of us all went mad in various ways, Emma remained steady. Unflappable and unjudgemental and very kind, and I was lucky to know someone like her. She was the centre of our group, the one everyone liked, and though over the years there were various fallings-out and resentments, Emma was never involved.

She had a kind of unambitiousness that made people comfortable around her. She never made you feel that she knew she was better than you, though she was better than all of us. She had this denim jacket that she wore right the way through the period of time when denim jackets were uncool, all the way up to when they became fashionable again.

Emma smoked like a chimney.

Emma laughed very loudly and generously, especially when a joke was at risk of falling flat.

Emma had, once, at a party when we were twenty-one, tried to kiss me, and I had laughed and kissed her on the cheek and said she didn't need to feel awkward about it. And she hadn't felt awkward, or hadn't seemed to. We had gone on just as we always had, loving each other as friends. She'd gone on to have girlfriends, never serious, never lasting for more than a few months. I, too, had gone on dates through my teenage years and later, though I had never committed to anything, finding it depressing somehow, the pressure to meet the demands of one person, the way you had to constantly make plans with them at the expense of your real life, and see less of your friends.

There was a round of Rock Paper Anything in which Emma played a ghost and I played the disapproval of one's parents and the conversation went round and round and round and nobody ever decided which of us should win.

After breakfast, we decided on a walk. It was something we'd always done in the old days, the kind of thing you felt you should do, go for a walk from your country hotel. Before, there had always been dogs, somebody or other always brought one, and Sam would pack us up a picnic that was too much and too fiddly, little brioche buns filled with crab and kimchi, bottles of homemade lemonade that were impractical to carry. Now it was just the four of us humans, Alicia clutching a takeaway cup of coffee from breakfast, and there was no focus other than the ground underfoot and each other. I missed the easy rhythms of the dogs weaving between us, the way conversation had to pause in order to summon them when they went too far ahead, the way they seemed to make things simpler and easier and to hold us all together. But it didn't matter, at least not at first. Conversation flowed. There was plenty to catch up on, after all. All those years of silence between us had been filled with our own lives. I pretended not to have googled them and so asked about their jobs, where they were living, that kind of thing, and I was genuinely curious about Emma, who didn't have an online presence. Nothing ever came up when I searched.

David talked about the law firm. Emma was head of geography at a school in Reading. Alicia was taking a break from consultancy work because of health issues, and she even spoke a little, seeming open and willing to share, about her struggles with anxiety and burnout, the toll it had taken on David, too. I knew about that, too, because she posted things on social media about the long road to recovery and wellness, pastel-coloured infographics about rest and healing.

'That's so hard,' Emma said. 'You guys are amazing.' And then, so easily, as if it wasn't a big deal, she reached out and squeezed first Alicia's shoulder and then David's, which was a small thing, a sweet gesture, but it seemed so natural between them that it took me aback. I began to notice, too, as the conversation ran on and the path sloped uphill, that they seemed to know more about each other than I knew about anything, and when David said, to Emma, 'How's Lottie?' I said, 'Who's Lottie?' and Alicia shot me a look and said, 'Her wife.'

'Oh, I didn't know,' I said. I could feel my face turning pink. 'That's wonderful, Em, congratulations.' And then, because I could tell already and because I was seized by an urge to press the bruise, I turned to David and Alicia and said, 'Were you guys at the wedding?'

Two, three, four paces through the mud and long grass before Alicia said, 'Yes. We were.'

'That's wonderful,' I said. 'Congratulations.'

I fell back a little bit and walked behind them, which I thought perhaps wasn't too strange; it was normal for people to shift and to stall on walks like that, wasn't it, to stop and gather your thoughts. My heart was beating very fast and I knew I had embarrassed myself. I had the thought that perhaps I should go back to the hotel, maybe leave altogether, get in my car and go home. It wasn't what I wanted, though. I wanted my friends back. I wanted my friends back. And so I kept walking behind them, and after a while Emma slowed her pace so she was next to me.

She was breathing heavily as we climbed.

'What's Lottie like?' I said.

'She's great,' said Emma. 'Thanks for asking.'

Footsteps. Panting. 'I'm glad,' I said.

'Shall we stop?' Emma said, and she stopped.

There was a fence at the edge of the path that she leaned against, her chest rising and falling. There wasn't much of a view from that particular spot, but I stood next to her and pretended to admire it anyway. She dug out her cigarettes and lit two in her own mouth, offering one to me. When I declined, she stubbed the spare one out on the fence post.

'Alicia says that what you're doing is brave,' said Emma, staring straight ahead. 'She says we should think that what you're doing is brave.'

'But what am I doing?' I asked. 'What am I doing that Alicia thinks is brave?'

Emma waved her cigarette around, gesturing vaguely at the sheep in the field beyond the fence, and the hills beyond the sheep and the clouds over the hills. 'Well, you know, asking us all here. I guess asking us all here so you can apologise.'

Alicia and David were some way ahead of us but they had stopped, too, and were gazing down at Emma and me, looking confused. David shouted something inaudible.

'I think I'll just head back, actually,' I said. 'I didn't sleep that well. I think I'll just head back to the hotel.' And I started walking back the way we'd come, which was downhill and so felt somehow inevitable, and I didn't stop to check whether the others had gone on without me or were still just standing there, or whether they were looking at me. And what was actually kind of amazing was that when I got back and my phone connected to the Wi-Fi, I'd received another email from Sam. It was identical to the previous one: 'JessicaBroder82, all the time you have spent alone can be enjoyed in the company of a lady that is pleased to be with you' and the link to the website of the hotel that I was, at that very moment, standing inside. And it was impossible, it didn't make any sense, that the Sam-spam could have alighted on the very hotel that had really been his, but then a lot of things were impossible, weren't they, the internet was impossible, Sam being dead in the first place was impossible, my friends thinking I had gathered them there to apologise, as though everything were my fault, impossible.

Sam threw a party for New Year's Eve. This was the winter before he died. He closed the hotel to outside guests so we had the run of the place. 'A night just for us,' Sam said, and there were fire pits out on the terrace, and of course he was roasting another hog, which made everything smell salty and sent the dogs so mad they had to be shut in the staff quarters. It wasn't quite my scene, which was odd to admit when all my closest friends were there, but the music was so loud. It was so dark I couldn't see exactly who was where or what they were doing, and people had brought other people, friends of friends, so it was busy and unfamiliar, and when Sam had said it would be a party just for us, I hadn't realised 'us' would include people I didn't know.

I went back to my room and crawled out onto the roof, listening to the music thudding up from below and looking out at the terrace, the firelight making everyone near it look golden and very lovely. They were getting louder as they got drunker; David and our friend Aidan were passing out shots of tequila. Emma was there and had brought a new girlfriend, Caroline, who she'd introduced me to that morning, and to whom I'd found myself unable to be nice, unable to be a normal, friendly friend. I had shaken Caroline's hand, which was too formal, and then said, 'Well, enjoy,' and gestured at the building which I knew was a weird thing to do. The two of them were by the fire pit, holding hands and smoking. I knew I was upset; I wasn't that oblivious to myself. I knew I wanted the hotel to be for me and my friends and nobody else. And I knew, too, that I wanted my friends to want that. I didn't like that they felt compelled to bring strangers here with them.

I knew this feeling was unacceptable.

'Knock knock,' Sam said, though he had already opened my door. 'Can I come in?' he said, as he came in. 'You okay?'

'Fine,' I said, wriggling back towards the open window to speak. 'Just taking a moment.'

'Are you sulking?' he said.

'A bit.'

'Thought so.'

His eyes looked blurry and he had a small smile stuck on his lips, which was typical of him when he was drunk. He came to the window and leaned out so the side of his body pressed against mine.

'What do you think of Caroline?' he said. He jutted his chin down to the terrace, where Caroline whispered something in Emma's ear and Emma laughed.

'I think Caroline's fine,' I said.

'Are you sulking about Caroline?' he said.

'A bit.'

His head fell on my shoulder and I had a sense of him, suddenly, as this enormous person, his enormous skull shockingly heavy, pressing into my neck. He rarely hugged people, had very rarely hugged me, and when he did he was stiff about it and ended it quickly. So this was unusual, welcome and pleasing, to feel close to him in that way. I wondered whether I should rest my head on his neck.

'We're all so lucky to have you, Sam,' I said.

'Sure,' he said.

'It's a wonderful party.'

'We're all kind of waiting,' he said, 'for you to decide. We've been waiting for you to decide for years and years and years.'

I could have said, 'Decide what?' but there was no need in that moment to pretend. Instead I said, 'I know.'

'If it's Emma, you just have to tell me. It would be fine, but you have to tell me.' He lifted his head to look at me. 'And you have to tell her, too.'

'I know,' I said, and felt lighter then, like we were in sight of dry land. 'I love you, Sam.' He didn't say it back, which was fine, I thought, more than fine, because who needs to say these things, really, and he leant forwards and kissed me, and I let him, thinking of the time Emma had done the same thing, and how afterwards it hadn't been awkward at all.

There was a round of Rock Paper Anything in which I played a rock and Sam played a rock.

The problem was that after the New Year's Eve party, it was in fact awkward with Sam. He had sent a few messages that almost but did not quite mention what had happened, *How are you doing, How are you feeling,* that kind of thing, and I had said I was excited for the next time we were all together at The Swan, and asked him about some expansion plans for the hotel he'd mentioned. He did not reply to my questions, and I didn't reply to his, and then when we were together in person he kept trying to meet my eye.

The other problem was that Caroline was always around. I hadn't had any issue with Emma's girlfriends, who had come and gone over the years, unmemorably, and I didn't have any issue specifically with Caroline, except that I was so stiff when she was around, uncomfortable and self-conscious, and she was suddenly always around. She was there when we met up for drinks in London, and she was there at birthday parties and at David and Alicia's engagement do, and she was there for all the subsequent visits to The Swan.

She learned to play Rock Paper Anything, beating Yasmin by playing a yeti against Jerusalem syndrome, beating our friend Ryan by playing the fear of the worst against scissors. Everyone acknowledged that Caroline was really very good at Rock Paper Anything. When it was my turn to face her, I played a sledgehammer and she played a computer virus, which sparked heated debate. Ultimately, I won because a sledgehammer could just smash the whole computer, couldn't it, could smash every computer until the virus was gone. This was before we really understood how much was, invisibly, controlled by computers.

I was aware that I was watching Emma and Caroline too intently. If I happened to come out of my room onto the mezzanine and see them below in the lobby, I would pause and wait for a while to see what they would do, to see how they were with each other when they thought they were alone. When they thought they were alone, they kissed. When they thought they were alone, Emma would lean back in her chair and rest her legs across Caroline's thighs and they would read their books or stare at their phones in silence. When they thought they were alone, Caroline would twist pieces of Emma's hair around her fingers. They did these things when they knew they were not alone, too.

Once, I was hovering on the mezzanine watching them when Aidan and David appeared behind me.

'Boo,' said David, and I jumped.

They stood next to me and saw what I was looking at.

'Oh, I see,' Aidan said. 'The lovebirds.'

'Disgusting,' David said, which was a joke I suppose, because he and Alicia were constantly being told to go back to their room.

'Yes,' I said, 'stomach-churning stuff.'

'Don't you want that for yourself one day, Jess?' said Aidan.

It wasn't an unusual thing, people asking me why I wasn't dating more, or why I'd never had a real partner, or whether I was asexual or what was going on there. I did always try to be honest and say that I just didn't mind that much, I already had everything I wanted, I loved my friends. But there was this sense among my friends that they needed to push me on it more, the comments were getting more frequent and more pointed. They had said things about friends not being enough, about friends just being part of your life and not all of it. And it wasn't like they didn't have a point. I had moments where I really did feel that I was jealous of Caroline, but the second I thought that I also thought how awful it would be if I did anything that risked my friendships with Emma, with Sam, with all of them. They were more important to me than anything, more important than sex, or love. My friends,

'It's getting a bit old, Jess,' said David. 'Maybe it's time to call off the dithering and loitering routine. You either want it or you don't. Not to mention Sam, poor sod, though I've told him enough times it's not worth waiting around for you.' He was annoyed, obviously, and being unfair. I chalked it up to the fact that he and Alicia were recently engaged, and perhaps he was getting cold feet.

Here's what happened. It was raining. Apocalyptic rain after several days of unbearable heat, and it meant we had been inside for the whole weekend. The dogs were restless and the people were restless. It was still too hot despite the downpour.

We had been drinking almost the whole day. Mimosas at breakfast. Prosecco through the morning while we played Scrabble. Beers with lunch. In the afternoon it was wine, and though I was quite good at holding my drink in those days, I was feeling it and so was everyone else. Sam said he had to go out to see a supplier, then returned a minute later saying he was in no state to drive and had cancelled the meeting. A few people went off to take naps and didn't reappear until the next morning, asking what happened, what happened, my God, what the hell happened.

We tried various things to entertain ourselves. We went outside to get drenched for a while, which wasn't as fun as it sounded. The smell of the mud was dense all around and when you breathed in the air was too wet, smothering. My soaked clothes clung to my body too tightly, and it felt as though somebody was gripping me. I went inside, got changed, and when I came back down, people had splintered off into small groups and I'd lost track of who was where, who'd gone to bed, who was still out in the rain. I think some people were watching a film in a nook up on the mezzanine. What I did know was that suddenly I was with Emma, and that Caroline was nowhere to be seen.

'Do you want a drink?' I said. She shook her head. 'Yeah, I've probably had too much too.'

We were in the lobby at a small table. Emma was twizzling an unlit cigarette in her fingers, occasionally tapping it against a coaster, and then said, 'Why don't you like Caroline?'

'I don't not like Caroline.'

'Don't lie.'

'I don't not like Caroline,' I said.

'What is it, then?' said Emma. 'Why don't you talk to me when she's around? Why don't you talk to her? You've been so weird.'

I shook my head.

'If it's just that you're jealous,' said Emma, 'which is what everyone is saying, then I don't understand why you never did anything, or said anything, when you had the chance.'

'Who is saying that I'm jealous?'

'Everyone is saying that.'

'What about now?' I said. 'Do I have the chance now?'

And, listen, I know it sounds wrong. If you think I haven't questioned myself in the years since, if you think I haven't considered my own intentions then you're wrong, of course, you're wrong. But I also know that my friends were always telling me to do something, were always pushing me to make up my mind, to call off the dithering. And part of what they were suggesting, surely, was something along the lines of what I did then, which was to lean towards Emma, towards where her elbow was pushed against the tabletop and then closer still, past her wrist and her fingers all the way until our lips were almost touching and I could smell the tobacco on her breath and feel the dampness of it, and then I kissed her.

I kissed Emma because I loved her, and my friends were always telling me to make up my mind. I kissed Emma because I loved Sam too, though in a different way, and had been led to believe by all of them that decisive action from me in this area of my life was a kindness to him, too. That was what I thought. That was what they had told me. They had repeatedly told me that, so how could they be angry about it, how could they blame me after the fact? I wanted to do the right thing. I wanted to do whatever was necessary to ensure we could all go on as we had before, happily, having a good time.

There was a heavy sound somewhere above us, a chair being pushed back suddenly; somebody stumbled on the mezzanine. We both looked up. We had the briefest glimpse of Sam, Aidan, Yasmin, maybe one or two others and heard someone saying, 'Sam,' but he was moving away and someone else said, 'Leave him. Give him some space.' The back of Sam's head, his shoulders, turning the corner towards the stairwell to the upper floors. A door slammed.

Then there was silence, Emma not meeting my eye and saying something sheepish about going to check on Caroline.

I sat there listening to the weather. Calm. Then shouts from outside and I went out to see what was happening and found that Sam was suddenly there on the terrace, our friends circling him, around his body, the rain. I think a guest, someone none of us knew, started screaming.

There was a round of Rock Paper Anything in which I played a rock again and Sam played a rock again, and it became a running joke within the running joke of the game, and he and I just played rocks every single time, until a time that must have been the last time, though we couldn't have known.

In the hotel, waiting for my friends to return from their walk, I thought about the nine years since Sam had died. The shock and the grief. The dreams that had persisted for a while in which he wasn't really dead, and the realisation each time upon waking that he was. The loss, in the aftermath, not just of Sam but of my dearest friends.

I hadn't replaced them, never socialised particularly, but when I did – when called upon to talk to people at a work party, or sometimes on dates – I spoke about my friends, about my wonderful friends, whom I had known my whole life, and I spoke about the good times we had at The Swan. It was almost showing off, the way I told it, and sometimes I caught myself and dialled it back a bit and said something about how we didn't see each so much these days, you know how it is, people had children, work, life gets in the way.

One time, I went to the pub with my colleagues at the publisher of medical journals and I told them about the game we played called Rock Paper Anything. I explained how funny it was, how unexpected and infinite the combinations, the joy of something that never makes sense but which was treated nonetheless as decipherable. Anything could happen, I said, you couldn't possibly begin to guess what. My colleagues listened politely and smiled and when I had finished, one of them said, 'Your friends sound like hard work, to be honest,' and a couple of other people laughed. What could I do but laugh with them, and nod, as though the burden of being friends with my friends was one I actually still bore?

And if my friends were correct in thinking, as it seemed they did, that the loss of Sam and the loss of the rest of them was my fault, what had I gained from it? What had been the purpose of all those years in which I knew, I did know, that things were complicated, that Emma harboured certain feelings towards me, that Sam did, and that the two of them and everyone else were waiting for me to do something about it? I had only wanted things to go on as they always had done. I had only wanted everything to stay the same, had done everything I did, and not done all the things I didn't do, with that goal in mind. They were such little things, kisses received or given; they were almost nothing.

And here, now, were David and Alicia and Emma coming into the hotel lobby, pink-cheeked from the fresh air and looking around for me and seeing me and coming closer, and closer. They were talking all at once and loudly; it seemed something had come unstoppered on their way back and now it was all flowing forth, everything they hadn't said to me ever since Sam had died.

'You were so lucky,' David was saying. 'You were this weird person who had nothing else going on, but he loved you, he adored you, and you didn't even have the decency to be grateful for that.'

'You must have known,' Alicia was saying, 'we spelled it out for you over and over, but you acted like you didn't.'

'I thought you'd apologise,' Emma said. 'But you've not even done that.'

'And why did you like us so much?' Alicia kept saying. 'What was it about any of us that made you like us so much?'

I let them finish, and when they did, I waited longer. I took a deep breath of the hotel air, that sweet whisky smell, woodsmoke, whatever it was they used to clean the floors. I knew there was no point wondering how it came to be that Sam's emails, which I understood, I did know, were random internet glitches, algorithmic witterings, had brought us back here. I knew it wasn't anything meaningful, that the messages had simply become tangled up in themselves and inadvertently summoned something that seemed like sense. The Swan. It was just Rock Paper Anything, infinitely arbitrary, and here we all were.

'But we were having such a good time,' I said. That was all there was, all I could say, whether or not it was enough. 'Weren't we? Weren't we having such a good time?'

The Innocents

Once we'd moved in, all Alice wanted to do was buy little things for our flat. She went into paroxysms over coasters, tea towels, candlesticks. 'Look,' she would say, waving her laptop at me one-handed, in a way that made me certain she'd drop it, 'look at this storage solution.' On the screen would be a little earthenware jar with a cork lid, or some sort of woven basket.

I couldn't understand it. Faced with the splintered floorboards and patchy paint job left behind by the previous owner, the leaking pipe under the kitchen sink that dripped into a yellow plastic box labelled 'MEDICAL WASTE DISPOSAL ONLY', my mind turned, if it turned at all, to sanders, plasterers and plumbers. When I mentioned these things to Alice, along with the likely associated costs, her attention wandered. She was interested only in festooning. Structural integrity did not concern her.

Our days: we stayed in the flat and ended up talking about it a lot. We stayed in the flat because we had to – it was during that period when you were allowed outside for a one-hour walk each day – but we would have wanted to stay in the flat anyway; it was so new, and we were so caught up in everything. We attended work meetings on Zoom. We sent emails and signed off, breezily, 'Stay safe!' Alice took up baking. We ate banana bread for breakfast, toasted with yogurt, and banana bread for lunch because why not. I assembled flat-pack bookshelves and then disassembled them because I'd put the slats on backwards.

Alice received an email from a wallpaper company suggesting their wallpaper would 'refine our confinement'. 'Must be a translation issue,' she said (the wallpaper company was Slovenian), 'confinement from the old French *confins*, meaning boundaries, from the Latin *confinium* meaning border or boundary limit, a shared border, i.e. wall. They just mean: spruce up yer walls,' she said. Then she added, 'The roots: *con-* meaning with, and *fin-* meaning end.'

'Refine your with-ends,' I said. I wasn't sure. I wasn't really engaged with any of it; confinement to me meant something else – two other things in fact – and besides, I was busy with other stuff.

What I was busy with was writing emails to our MP. Once you've written more than one email to your MP in a reasonably short period of time – a fortnight, say – the game becomes: how not to seem like a crazy person. I became a student of the genre. How long should an email be? How formal or familiar? Should I link to scientific papers supporting my argument, or would that suggest paranoia? How many citations per email is too many? Was I a crazy person?

We had started trying to buy the flat almost a year before we moved in. The process had been slow, in part because of us (we worried about money, about rising damp, about whether we would like the new neighbourhood as much as we liked the area where we rented) and mostly because the seller kept changing her mind about things, like whether or not she wanted to sell us the flat. All we knew about her was that she was a single woman who had lived there with her husband, and then they had divorced and she had lived there alone. The estate agent had told us this as though it was quite an exciting story. By the time the sale went through, lockdown had started and the people from the removal company had to social-distance from each other, taking turns to carry in our boxes, trying not to breathe each other's air.

The flat only really had three rooms: two bedrooms (one big, one small) and an open-plan kitchen-living room with French windows onto a little courtyard garden that was overlooked by much larger houses on the street that ran parallel to ours. The smaller room, we said, would be the baby's. The bathroom was downstairs in the basement, which was dark and damp and made us both a little anxious. Still, there was something reassuring about it all, even the damp; it felt solid and old in a way that made us seem insignificant, and therefore made all the things we worried about seem less worrying.

We were able to buy the flat thanks to a large gift from Alice's father, which he had made thinking she was buying the place alone. We had put my name alongside hers on the deed all the same. On our first day, once the movers had left, I wandered between the three rooms feeling that I had somehow stolen them from Alice's father, who disliked that

Alice was gay, and to whom Alice had never mentioned our relationship, saying it was easier for everyone, that this way nobody had to say what they were thinking.

The other feeling I had on that first day was a sort of horror, because the previous owner had left the whole place in a state of such disarray that even I, chronically messy according to Alice and extremely unobservant according to everyone, was horrified: there were piles of paperwork abandoned in corners, a broken bedstead in the bath; there was a half-eaten banana in the sink and a smell of iodine that permeated every room, even the basement. The dog ran through the place making a sort of gasping, panting sound, though her tail was wagging and she didn't seem distressed. Later, when she calmed down, she curled up on the floorboards in the corner of what was going to be the baby's room.

We filled bin liners with the previous owner's detritus and lit scented candles to drown out the smell. There were a lot of tablets wedged between the floorboards. 'Vitamins,' I said, and Alice said, 'Drugs.' The stacks of paper were mostly bills; a lot of them were from a company called Bioanalysis4U. Some of them were for things like window-cleaning and electricity.

'Welcome home,' said Alice, though she said it while gazing intently at an invoice for blood plasma tests, so it seemed like she was welcoming the invoice home rather than me, or us.

I had this feeling all the time that something awful was about to happen. It was so very quiet and strange, nobody coming or going, nobody knowing how long it would go on like this. Those early days in the flat had an air of finality about them, as though we were never again going to live so simply or so peacefully. As though we would look back on them and say, 'God, we were so innocent, so ignorant, so stupid.' We would seem, to our future selves, to have been refining our confinement and eating banana bread just moments before the whole place blew up or slipped under water. I took it upon myself to say, 'God, we are so innocent, we are so stupid,' out loud, as though, in demonstrating my self-knowledge, I would be less so.

Alice looked up from her phone, bemused. She thought I was saying 'indolent' and I corrected her but she remained bemused even then. She was buying a set of six slate coasters hand-painted with wildflowers from someone who described themselves online as a 'maker and mystic'. Alice was entertained by the idea of mystic coasters.

'God, we are so innocent,' I said.

Then the previous owner texted us saying she still had a set of keys she forgot to hand over. The estate agent had given her our numbers, she said, which felt like something that shouldn't happen. She signed off the message with her full name, 'regards from Libby Crewe', as though it was an email or a letter. We said she should drop them through the letterbox. She said she would and then went silent. Alice and I admitted to each other that we felt uneasy about this – Libby Crewe, the keys – so we called a locksmith, who said he wasn't supposed to be taking on jobs but would help us if we kept a safe distance. He changed the locks. We stood well back. We felt better afterwards, though we couldn't do anything about the main entrance to the building, which we shared with the two flats above us. Libby Crewe's set of keys would still work in that lock.

I was writing to our MP because we had two frozen embryos in storage at a fertility clinic, and we were being told we were not allowed to use them. The fertility clinic had been forcibly closed – temporarily, the letter we'd received had stressed – pending an investigation for medical malpractice and negligence, and no activity could take place during this time. That meant no treatments, and it also meant that they were unable to send our frozen embryos to a different clinic; the whole place was on ice and had been for six months. Now there was a lockdown and everywhere else was on ice, too. There appeared to be no end in sight and my complaints, at first informal, then formal, then increasingly furious and therefore less formal again, had gone unanswered.

Our MP promised to look into it and then went quiet. I sent her pdfs of articles about the correlation between age and unsuccessful IVF treatments, arguing that with every passing week our chance to have a family diminished. I was thirty-four and though I knew I was not about to become barren the second I turned thirty-five, I felt that the graph showing the steep decline in successful outcomes was a compelling part of my case. Sometimes I stared at the graph and despite myself felt a sort of vertigo at the line's sharp drop. Sometimes I wrote 'our right to have a family' instead of 'our chance'. I sent our MP links to news reports about court cases that involved situations similar to ours. Once, I wrote a detailed description of the clinic, of how professional and normal it had seemed, and how we had thought its relative affordability was simply down to a limited-time-only special offer we had found advertised online.

It had seemed so clean and bright there, I said. We had gone in full of trepidation, worried about how we would ever afford it, worried about what the process would do to our bodies, worried that it wouldn't work. But the doctor had been so kind, had listened to our medical histories and made her recommendations in clear, comprehensible language. It was very convincing.

We asked about the special offer we'd seen online and the doctor said yes, new patients planning to use donor sperm could receive treatment at roughly half price, so long as they were willing to buy from the clinic's preferred sperm bank. This had not struck us as strange, one sperm seeming very like another, the donors listed in the catalogue as bland and interchangeable as people on the Tube. It all seemed completely innocent.

Now we were being told that the clinic had failed to cap the number of babies per donor (the legal limit was ten) and while we had no idea how many babies *our* donor had created, an investigation was being carried out. I pictured siblings in their hundreds wandering around the city, unwittingly bumping into each other at nursery, in the soft-play area, then growing up to run into each other in Starbucks or sit next to each other on the bus, ignorantly.

When I imagined our children, snuggled icily together in a Petri dish in a cordoned-off freezer in the forbidden clinic, I wondered how many siblings they had, and whether I had ever seen them.

I was adamant, regardless, that we had the right to our own embryos, that we should not be prevented from accessing them, that our children had effectively been kidnapped, that the clinic had no right to do this. This was the gist of my emails to the MP.

Everybody I spoke to about this was absolutely certain I was in the wrong, except Alice. Everyone said something along the lines of, 'But why would you want to have children who have God-knows-how-many unknown siblings?' I said, 'None of us know how many siblings we have. Not really.' I also said, 'Ignorance is bliss.' Alice was supportive but attempting to distract us both from the stress of it all with fabric swatches for cushion covers.

Alice said she heard someone trying their keys in our front-door lock during the night. There had been scratching, the hinges rattling, and then a loud, huffy sigh. I said it must have been a dream.

A week or so later, we became aware that someone was stealing our post. The way the post worked was that it came through the main front door of the building, and whichever of the residents came across it first would sort it into trays in the shared hallway. We knew someone was taking ours because *The New Yorker* came every week, and then it didn't.

'Maybe we forgot to tell them our new address?' Alice said, which was not a helpful suggestion, since we had received the magazine as normal the first three weeks, and I had a vivid memory of the arcane processes I'd followed to update our details, which had involved spending a lot of time on the phone to a friendly American call-centre worker called Brian. Brian had politely insisted that our old address had been in the Netherlands, and that unless I could confirm the Dutch address he couldn't input the new one. In the end, he told me what the Dutch address was and I confirmed it, and *The New Yorker* arrived at the new flat.

Anyway, someone was stealing our post.

The flat directly above us belonged to a man called Roger who was a celebrity security guard. We knew he was a celebrity security guard because his letters came addressed to a company name that we googled; it was a protection agency for famous people. Roger's face was on the website. He looked, in the photo, both bigger and more menacing than he did in real life; when we saw him in person it was always as he was returning from a jog, sweaty and pink and staggering up the path to the front door, panting. He was allergic to dogs, he said, but he always wanted to pet ours when he saw her; he pulled his collar up over his mouth and his sleeve down over his hand to pat her head.

Above Roger there was an old lady whom we almost never saw. The mail she received was mainly catalogues printed on very thin, slippery paper.

We didn't think either Roger or the old lady were responsible for stealing the post. We felt, both of us, a troubling kind of certainty that it was Libby Crewe who was doing it, though we could think of no motive and had no evidence at all.

'I hope she's enjoying *The New Yorker*, at least,' I said, but Alice thought she was probably just flicking through to find the cartoons.

I imagined the issues stacking up on Libby Crewe's coffee table. The surface of our own coffee table was now disconcertingly clear.

It was possible that letters bearing news about our stolen embryos were being stolen. It was possible that letters bearing very bad news were being stolen, and we knew nothing about it. 'Or very good news,' Alice said, but neither of us believed that.

The chances of having a live birth (this is what the clinic called it) after the transfer of a single frozen embryo were (the clinic said) one in four. This was as likely as tossing a coin twice and getting tails both times. The odds declined to one in six once the patient was older than thirty-five, which was like throwing a six the first time you rolled a dice.

I was intrigued by probability at the time, couldn't stop thinking about it: what was likely, what was unlikely, what would happen despite its unlikeliness. I looked at gambling websites, trying to make sense of the odds they listed on which horse was likely to run faster than the other horses. I felt tempted sometimes to place bets on things like that, which horse or team of rowers or race car would end up being the fastest one, and then instead I spent money on flowers for Alice. There was a very fashionable florist nearby who spray-painted the foliage to make everything even brighter than it already was.

'How long will this last, do you think?' said Alice, and she could have meant the deliveries of painted flowers, or the lockdown, or the extent to which we worried about Libby Crewe.

'If something bad happens to you,' I said to Alice, 'no matter how unlikely it was that it would happen, the chances of it having happened to you are one hundred per cent.'

'That's a very disturbing thing to say,' said Alice, but I hadn't meant it in a horrifying way, just that I worried all the time that the things I worried about would really happen.

I woke at 2 a.m. to the sound of somebody trying our lock. Scratching, rattling, a muffled 'Ugh.' I lay in bed completely rigid, and my heart beat so loudly it almost drowned out the noises at the door. I knew I should get up and see who or what was trying to get in, but I couldn't bring myself to move, and then, after a while, it was quiet again. I told Alice about it in the morning over banana bread. The next night she heard it and I didn't.

Both explanations seemed increasingly likely: that Alice and I were passing a dream back and forth, a nightmare that had taken hold of both of us at once; that Libby Crewe was returning in the night to steal our post and try her key in our lock.

We read online that post deliveries were disrupted in our area because of ongoing staffing issues at the local sorting office.

One day we received a single letter, addressed to Libby

Crewe. We opened it, even though, having googled, we knew this was considered theft. We told ourselves it was reasonable because we didn't have a forwarding address for her and because she kept trying to break into our flat. The letter said bailiffs were coming to collect an unpaid debt to a medical-testing company.

We awaited the arrival of the bailiffs as a potentially exciting event: what would we say; how would we explain; what would they try to take from us?

Now, whenever the doorbell rang, we thought it might be them, or if not them then Libby Crewe dropping off her keys, but it was only ever couriers asking us to sign for packages on behalf of Roger, the celebrity security guard, who was out more than he was strictly allowed to be.

Now, whenever either of us heard someone trying our lock in the night, we thought it might be Libby Crewe, but we also thought it might somehow be the bailiffs come to collect her unpaid debt – and sometimes, around 3 or 4 a.m., when I couldn't sleep but couldn't wake up fully enough to snap out of it, I thought it might be Alice's father trying to catch me in the act of sleeping beside his daughter. When I was really more asleep than awake I thought it might be our frozen babies, having escaped their Petri dish, trying to find their way home, and what was awful was that in those moments I was scared of the children, terrified; those ice-babies were no more welcome than any of the other people I feared might be trying to come in.

*

Neither Alice nor I admitted to being terrified of the scratching sounds at our door at night because we were both trying to be the strong one. But I noticed that Alice would jump and sometimes even scream when I walked unexpectedly into a room she was in. And once, when it started to rain heavily and suddenly, making a clatter against the windows, I was so shocked that for a moment I could not breathe.

Dear Libby Crewe, Alice texted. *Just wondering when you might be able to drop off the keys? Also do you have a forwarding address?* We didn't hear back.

Alice hired a wallpaper-stripping machine from an appliance-rental company and spent three days steaming and scraping Libby Crewe's wallpaper from our bedroom walls. There was a very specific smell when she did this: the old heated-up wallpaper glue, the damp mountain of torn-up paper amassing at the foot of the stepladder, pearly and limp. The plaster underneath was in bad condition; it flaked off when touched. In a corner, Alice uncovered 'LIBBY CREWE' written in thick white paint inside a dripping heart.

We painted the whole room terracotta, and for a while that's the colour it stayed. Then Alice said it was all wrong and ordered wallpaper from the Slovenian wallpaper company. The paper, when it arrived, was incredibly beautiful – even nicer than it had looked online.

I tried to repair the boiler, but in the end we had to pay someone else to do it. The same thing happened with the washing machine, but I did manage to fix the leaking sink myself. All of this, the repairs, the wallpaper, was expensive.

I looked again, wistfully, at the gambling websites, and cut back on the bouquets of painted flowers.

Alice painted the baby's room a pessimistic blue, and the skirting boards pale grey. I dug tablets out from between the floorboards with a paring knife.

We couldn't afford a new oven, so we made do with the one that Libby Crewe had left behind, even though it got so hot on the outside that we both injured ourselves. I had an em-dash burn across my shin from walking into the open door while Alice was taking out a fresh loaf.

When we talked about the embryos it was only in practical terms: about who to write to next, and what to try, and whether we should contact a lawyer, even though we knew we would never be able to afford it. 'Citizens Advice Bureau?' Alice suggested. 'A petition?' We didn't talk about what we would do if it didn't work out, if the baby room was never occupied by a baby, in the same way we didn't talk about what we would tell Alice's father if it *did* work out, about how, if ever, she was going to announce that not only did I exist, but that she and I were making more of us together.

If the baby room was never occupied by a baby, I knew I would have to find a way to make us both happy with a different life to the one we had both hoped for. I knew Alice felt the same thing, that it would be up to her to make sure we were all right; we both had this habit of thinking we were the responsible one. I thought perhaps we'd end up having a lot of dogs. I wrote again to our MP, explaining about Alice, about how much I wanted her to be happy. I explained that all of this would have been less painful if we didn't love each other so much.

If you're wondering why I am writing in fits and starts like this, it's because the baby keeps waking up and needing things, which tells you everything you need to know about how this story goes, or at least the headline – though Alice, reading over my shoulder, posits 'punchline'. The story ends with us getting compensation from the unscrupulous fertility clinic and our frozen embryos vanishing into the void. Or at least this is how it felt; I'm not sure what really happened to the embryos; perhaps they simply threw the whole Petri dish away.

The story ends, too, with Libby Crewe fading from our thoughts and our flat, our nights falling silent and then filling up with other sounds as the lockdown eased and the world began again. We would hear people outside on the street walking noisily back from the pub, and traffic sounds, and music, and nobody tried their key in our lock any more. It was surprising how quickly we forgot how scared of her we had been, and sometimes I doubted that we had heard what we thought we had heard. Alice stopped jumping when I entered the room and I was no longer afraid of loud rain.

The story ends with Alice and I going to an above-board clinic and beginning the process all over again and our coin-toss giving us tails twice in a row. But the problem was, neither of us knew that would happen before it happened, and we didn't know what would happen with the flat either, or with its previous owner, or any of the other things we worried about.

The doorbell rang and Alice said, 'I bet it's Libby Crewe,' even though we were both fully expecting it to be a courier with a package for Roger, but when we answered it was a woman in a suit that didn't quite fit her. She was a little out of breath, as though she had sprinted to us, and when she opened her mouth to speak the first thing that came out was a cough. Eventually she told us that she was a bailiff, and I wanted to kick myself for having anticipated the bailiff so constantly and then, in the key moment, forgetting to anticipate her. Alice pulled the two of us forwards and shut the front door behind us, because she had read online that bailiffs were not allowed to force entry. The woman looked unsurprised and just asked, calmly, whether one of us was Libby Crewe. We said no, that she no longer lived here – we were talking over each other and too quickly, as though we were lying – and I waited for the bailiff to roll her eyes, to say, 'Pull the other one,' to say, 'Sure, sure, of course you're not her.'

Instead she simply nodded, got out her phone and typed something on it, and said, 'Do you have her new address?'

We said we did not. The bailiff thanked us. She tucked her phone back in her pocket and walked off down the street. Alice and I paused, waiting for the fight we'd been sure would ensue, which we'd discussed and imagined at length, in which the bailiff tried to break down our door and we asserted that this was illegal and called the police. After a moment, we turned to go back inside.

The problem was that neither of us had a key and now we were locked out, so we had to call the locksmith again. The locksmith made us wait on the pavement while he tried the trick they do with the credit card, but when that failed he had to drill, and we had new locks fitted for a second time. All this time we had been worrying about people breaking in, and in fact the only people who had broken in so far were me and Alice.

The doorbell rang, and we both bet that it was Libby Crewe, but Alice was in the middle of hanging curtains in the baby's room – she had found rolls of fabric on the pavement outside a neighbour's house with a label saying 'PLEASE TAKE', and had made them herself – so I went to the door alone.

I knew the man waiting outside was Alice's father because I had met him once years earlier, before Alice and I moved in together. He had arrived unannounced at her flat, much like he was arriving unannounced now, and I had been only partially dressed. Alice had explained me away: a friend whose shower wasn't working.

I couldn't tell from his expression whether Alice's father remembered me. He stared. Perhaps he didn't recognise me with trousers on. I began concocting plausible reasons why I was there, all of which seemed in the moment unconvincing at a time when none of us were supposed to be anywhere other than our own homes.

'Oh,' he said, 'I was hoping it would be you.'

I nodded as though I understood. He held out one of those

tall gift bags made for wine bottles, and I could see inside it, right at the bottom, was a wooden bird.

'It's an ornament,' he said. 'House-warming. I think it's a collared dove. Maybe a cuckoo.' Then he bent forwards in an odd little bow and said, 'For both of you.'

'Shall I get Alice?' I asked, and then remembered to say, 'Thank you.'

But Alice's father shook his head and insisted he wasn't staying, was just stopping by to drop off the gift, and that it was me he had hoped to see. 'She thinks I don't know about all this,' he said, waving a hand at whatever he imagined was going on in the flat behind me, although maybe it was just at me. 'I thought at first she'd tell me, so I could reassure her. But she hasn't told me, so I haven't been able to reassure her. If you can find a way to stop her worrying,' he said, 'perhaps you could.'

'Would you like to come in?' I said. 'She's hanging some curtains.'

'No, no, not allowed,' he said, and did another little bow.

Back inside, I put the wooden cuckoo in the baby's room and wondered whether her father had meant anything by the cuckoo specifically and wondered how and when to tell Alice that things were not as bad as she had thought they were, that in this regard they were pleasant even – but this too would be unnerving to find out, and I wasn't sure how to broach it.

'People change, you know,' Alice's father had said on the doorstep, and in the moment he said it I thought it was a kind of threat. Only later did I realise he had meant to put me at ease.

*

When the baby cries, he looks exactly like Alice – so like her that sometimes I want to run and comfort her as well as him, and then I find her sitting peaceably on the sofa, smiling at something on her phone or stretching out her arms to take him from me, and suddenly I am overwhelmed almost to the point of needing comfort myself because how can it be that this world is the world we live in, and that I get to live in it with the two of them? It feels almost too much, too implausibly much.

The doorbell rang – Libby Crewe? we both went to see – but this time, it was two policemen in uniform, tall and blocking the light. Not long before, part of my brain would have thought they were there because of the unpaid medical-testing bill, or even some dreadful thing I had done and then forgotten I'd done. Or I would have thought: Alice's father has sent them to arrest me for living here with his daughter. Or even: perhaps our MP has become tired of all my letters and has sent them to tell me off about it. Now, steadily, bad possibilities were falling away. What some distant and crazy part of my brain did think was: these two policemen are my children, having escaped the Petri dish in the freezer, trying to find their way home.

The dog was excited at the prospect of visitors, nosing the backs of our knees, trying to get past us to see them.

The policemen asked whether Libby Crewe was in the house.

Alice and I looked at each other and I knew we were both thinking: *God, I hope not.*

'No,' said Alice, 'she doesn't live here any more. We live here now.'

The police said Libby Crewe had been seen wandering around the neighbourhood, trying her keys in people's doors and then running away. The police had been called, but by the time they arrived she had vanished. Neighbours who recognised her had given them her name and this address.

'We thought – we did actually think – that she was trying to break in here too,' said Alice.

The policemen asked whether we had Libby Crewe's new address, and we said we did not, but we gave them her phone number.

They looked like they were going to leave, but suddenly we found we couldn't stop talking about Libby Crewe; all this stuff just came pouring out of us, about the tablets in the floorboards and the unpaid bills and 'MEDICAL WASTE DISPOSAL ONLY' and about our missing post and the shared dream that couldn't be just a dream, about the way she had failed to get into the flat but had nonetheless crept inside our brains almost as soon as we arrived and given us this sensation all the time that something dreadful was about to happen, about the bailiff. The policemen looked mildly intrigued, entertained even, and I think we would have kept going like that, just talking and talking, mentioning even the white heart painted under the wallpaper, and I would have brought up the embryos too before long, about how you could say they had been kidnapped, but before we had a chance the dog slipped past us and danced jubilantly around and between the policemen's legs and jumped up, front paws on their thighs.

By the time we got her back inside, the policemen had left. They had told us not to worry and that they would get in touch with Libby Crewe and put a stop to the night-time visits, and suddenly Alice started to cry, to really sob, her face creasing up and reddening, almost magenta against the dark blue of the baby's bedroom walls, her eyes invisible, crying and crying and crying, not talking about relief or about all the things that could have been bad and weren't, but saying instead, 'But what if we don't ever feel at home here,' and saying, 'But what if it's never more than just the two of us,' and saying, 'But what if things aren't going to be okay.'

And all I could do was look from the back of the door we had closed to the dog to the blue walls to the mystic slate coasters arranged on a side table so that it looked to me in that moment like a six on the face of a dice, and then to the wooden bird her father had brought and then to Alice and say, 'But what if we do, what if it is, what if it will be, what if they are?'

Acknowledgements

Thanks –

to my agent, Rebecca Carter at Rebecca Carter Literary, who has been steadfast and brilliant and hopeful across the many years it took to write these stories,

to my editor, Sophie Missing, at Scribner UK, for insight and patience and care,

to Emma Parry at Janklow and Nesbit in the US, who sees my work clearly and has been generous to it, and to me,

to Jill Bialosky, my editor at Norton, for her wisdom,

to Tilda Butterworth at Rebecca Carter Literary, clear-sighted and kind,

to everyone at Scribner and at Norton who helped these stories find their shape and place in the world,

to the writers who have encouraged, advised, inspired, consoled and cajoled me across years of work, including Daisy Johnson, Tom Lee and Laura Marris,

to Claudia Gray, Grace Shortland and Amanda Walker, for the good times,

to Margaret and Richard Stevens, always,

to Ambrose and Aphra Williams: the beginnings and

hoped-fors and counterarguments and interruptions of these stories,

and to Eley Williams, who shows me how it's done.